The FOX
And The Falcon

DEE CAREY

Writers' Branding
1-800-608-6550
www.writersbranding.com
orders@writersbranding.com

Contents

*To my late husband Bill
and my deceased doxie Widget.
Save a place for me, guys.
I love and miss you.*

Acknowledgments

Couldn't do this without my critique partner, Steve Yates.

Introduction

On my way to Camelot, I saw my friend Merlin, and he did not look happy. Had he noticed the change? He appeared to be chastising someone. As he was red faced with anger.

Without warning, pain shot through my left wing. When I looked back, I saw Merlin shaking a lanky boy as he held him by the front of his tunic, a small pile of stones at his feet. The wizard lifted the lad, his shoes dangling in midair as he squirmed to be released. Good, that will teach the rapscallion to throw stones at creatures of the wild.

Chapter 1

Merlin

"I swear, Arthur, I've never met as an unruly a being as that boy Finn, who spends his time at the marshes."

"What is there to do in the marshes that would interest a young boy?" the King asked.

"Well, Sire, I've seen him there for several days. He seems to enjoy throwing small rocks at living things, ducks, falcons, even the occasional fox. I've warned him, but he persists."

"He's a strange lad. Ever since his father was made a baron, he's been a thorn in my side. I've received many requests from the villagers to stop harassing their livestock. The boy obviously thinks he has immunity from whatever foul deed, he commits. I believe he's done far worse than thrown stones at unwary creatures."

Though I was involved in thinking about this evil lad, I was also well aware the King did not appear to be his usual robust self. His color was almost grey, even his eyes were grey, lacking any brightness at all. He sat up and leaned back on his pillows as I moved to his bedside. I leaned over him and gently placed my hand on his neck. It was hot.

"Arthur, how are you feeling? You appear to have a fever."

"Frankly, Merlin, I haven't felt well for about a week now."

This is strange. In about that same amount of time, several folks from the castle have come to me with the same symptoms. It is spring, and we rarely have so many become ill. I will oversee the meals for a few days. Perhaps something there was tainted.

~ ~ ~

Morganna

"Damnation, why do I feel so ill? I can't ever recall feeling so sick. I can barely raise my head from the pillow, but I must, as I feel Lady Elaine approaching."

She is so imperious. She's not only a priestess, she thinks she is the greatest priestess who ever served on Avalon. Elaine is old, yet she retains her youthful beauty. But I've been on the isle longer than her. She merely set a foot on Avalon and without learning a single ritual, she is made Grand High Priestess. I guess all it takes is money.

"Morganna, pay attention. Do you need a healer? Are you hungry or thirsty?" she asked in her usual haughty manner.

No, I just want you to go away. However, it is not wise to speak to a High Priestess in this manner.

"I don't feel the need of a healer, though a drink from the well would be welcome."

"Of course, my dear I shall fetch it at once."

Having said that she flounced from my quarters, the panels of her gown drifted in the gentle breeze, appearing as wings. First, she sends me to the isle when I had just learned to walk, makes me learn the entire history of Avalon, makes me know each and every ritual and forces me to ascend each order. Then when she can't stand her husband, she comes here and changes everything. The rules that stood for centuries, no longer pertain to the High Priestess.

My quarters are very nice, but they were once home to far more sumptuous things. The rooms that were once assigned to me overlooked the sacred lake and afforded a spectacular view. The bed covers were made of the finest silk. My gowns were sewn with gold thread. I was only days away from my installation, as High Priestess, when "she" arrived, and nothing seemed as it had always been. For centuries the rules, rituals, and knowledge of the history of Avalon served as the hallmark of the isle. Now all of it, gone. How? And more importantly, why?

~ ~ ~

Finn (New baron's son)

I wish we were back home. I hate it here. There is nothing to do, can't ride we didn't bring my horse, can't fish in the lake, it's sacred. Don't they know ducks, fish, and even dogs foul it? All I want to do is swim.

Why does that old mage watch me all the time? *Not today, you ancient fool. Today is mine. I will create such havoc, they will send me home.*

Quietly I left the meadow, these mindless women favored. Swiftly, I clung to the few shadows until I was free of the ivory palace. I know it was forbidden to leave alone. Here everyone must disclose their whereabouts, so you were never alone.

Well, you little sheep, today this lamb will escape and do as he choose.

I went around the lake to the distant marsh where grew all types of tall grasses. Sitting among the rushes, I knew I could not be seen.

The warmth of the sun, the solitude, and the quiet, relaxed me and I fell asleep. When I woke the sun was at its zenith. Yet, I have not been seen, for I am sure if I were, someone would report me. This place is like a dungeon.

I moved closer to the water and picked up some pebbles. At first, I threw the flatter ones and watched them skip across the sacred lake. But, that was boring.

My boredom passed when a flock of mallards landed near the marsh. I took a small but sharp pebble from my pile, threw, and hit the drake, sending the congregation flying. Now, this is fun.

Damn, I finally get to enjoy myself and along comes the nosey wizard.

I didn't have the time or the space to run. The marsh ahead of me is soft, and the path behind me was too narrow to race and I will sink deep into the muck. The old man is far lighter than I and he crossed the marsh in seconds. He might be light and frail, but he is far stronger than I imagined. He grabbed me by the front of my tunic and lifted me higher than he was tall, shaking me until the marrow in my bones tingled.

"Boy," he shouted. "Do you think just because your father is now a baron, you can do as you please? Not so, lad, not so. Everyone must abide by the rules."

The only way to get him to release me was to capitulate.

"I'm sorry, Sir, I'll not do it again. I promise."

"Do you truly comprehend? Any further misdeed will place you in grave danger. Understand?"

"I understand. You shall never again have reason to chastise me."

Merlin then lowered me to the ground. I stood before him trying to look very contrite.

"I'll let it pass, just this once. I'd better not catch you again."

The ancient mage glared at me. *You'll not catch me again, old man. I'll just be more careful the next time.*

~ ~ ~

Chuck (ground hog)

Don't wander too much this away, but I ain't seed my old friend Fiona fer sum time. So I walks inter the marsh as fur as I dares. This part of the marsh will hold me cuz it ain't too mushy. Still it ain't one a my favorites. Keeps achangin all the time. A fellar has ter be most careful.

Wall hows about thet? Thar she is, I said to myself. She shore is a purty bird, them feathers on her back are shiney, most like the King's own robe. I'ma guessin ya don't call feathers a coat, but this particular bird has one dad burned beautiful hide.

I lifted my paw in greetin and she lands jest aside me. *I knows a fellar like me would never have a chance, but dang she's elegant, smart as a whip and kind. Guess thet is what makes her so lovable.*

"Hi, Fiona, watcha doin in these parts? Ain't seed ya in a while."

She shook her feathers and preened em back in place. It were kinda breezy so I guess they got messed up some.

"Hi, Chuck," she replied, "I've been doing some investigating for Merlin. I saw him here a few days past. The wizard was very angry. He caught a young lad throwing stones at falcons and ducks."

"I knows, I seed him too. Right foolish fellar. It ain't smart to make a wizard mad."

"Quite unwise indeed. Have you seen him since then?"

"Nope. Why? Are ya lookin' fer em?"

"Not really, I've come to see Morganna. A small bird told me she was ill."

"Yeah, I heered thet too. Let me know hows she's doin will ya?"

"Of course, my friend," she said, and opened them soft lovely, wings and flies toward Camelot.

~ ~ ~

Fiona

The castle is strangely quiet. The servants are completing their tasks in silence. The few knights are eating without their utensils striking the plate. No one is speaking to anyone. The silence is like a cacophony of insects at dusk.

I pumped my wings gently to avoid making noise. As I flew off the main corridor, I noticed Morganna's door was a jar and sounds of vomiting emanated. I entered and saw a vision I never expected. Morganna was leaning over the side of the bed emptying the contents of her stomach into a basin.

I perched on her bedpost and waited until she raised her head and wiped her mouth with the back of her hand. She pushed her hair back saying, "Fiona, I'm so sick. I never get sick. Why? Why? Why am I so sick?"

I flew down to her side and extended my wing over her shoulder. She leaned into me and sobbed. I had no idea why she despaired, or what I could do to ease her. I helped her to lie back and she cried herself to sleep. Knowing she was safe, I left. There had to be a way to heal her.

I flew through the cavernous hallways until I came upon Merlin's quarters. I entered and saw the old man was pouring over a huge tome, running his finger down the page. It was covered in the finest leather and smelled of mold.

"Merlin," I asked, "I've not seen this book before. Why do you study it so intently?"

"Ah. Little Fiona, I search for medicine to cure the king."

"Cure the king? What illness has befallen him?"

"That, my dear, is what I hope to learn."

"How long has the king been ill?"

"He tells me he hasn't been well for a week." I nodded.

"This is the same period Morganna has been sick. She is very concerned, as she is rarely afflicted with even the most minor of illnesses. She has been vomiting for days. I only left her as she cried herself to sleep."

Merlin turned from the book and pulled on his long, white beard as he was wont to do as he ponders an issue of grave concern.

The great wizard swirled, his cape snapping in the wind, his demeanor was one I never before witnessed. There was fear in his countenance. The most renowned sorcerer through the entire world was afraid!

"How many are now ill?" he asked. His eyes darted all about the room.

"Fiona, Fiona, we could well have an epidemic on our hands."

"I understand, Master Merlin, what can I do to aid you?"

The old man began to chant, very rapidly. I did not understand the language, so I did not know what I was expected to do.

Finally, he lowered his arms and began to speak. Again, I did not understand. Then his speech began to slow, and I understood. He'd been using English all along, but at a speed that was incomprehensible. He came back to the man he was before the chant and addressed me.

"Fiona, my girl, I leave it to you to find how many are ill, how many, if any, died and if there is there a commonalty among the stricken. I realize it is a task of monumental proportions, but you have talents you have not yet discovered."

~ ~ ~

Merlin

Nothing really has changed in the last week except the unruly Finn. I know he is wild, but I don't think he's evil. Just the usual adolescent rebellion. But I will check it out just in case.

As I arrived at the marsh, I saw no one. Even the ducks were missing. Then I heard a rustling in the reeds and from the rushes emerged Fiona's friend Chuck. He was an olde soul, and the most selfless being I have ever met.

"Good day, Sir Chuck," I said, raising my hand in greeting. He looked up, stopped chewing on an apple, and waved.

I began to search the area for any signs of Finn. Apparently, the lad has found something to torment other than ducks and falcons. There was no sign of him.

I felt a slight pull on my robe. Perhaps I'd caught it on something. Looking down I saw Chuck holding the hem of my garment.

"Whatcher yer doin in these parts, Master Wizard?"

"You needn't be so formal, Chuck. We've been friends for years. Merlin will suffice."

"Wall, I jest think a feller should be speckted for his talent."

"That is most kind of you. And is much appreciated. Can you tell me if you've seen young Finn today? You know, the boy who likes throwing stones."

"Naw, ain't seed him in couple days back."

~ ~ ~

Finn

That fool wizard thinks he can best me. Well, he is mistaken.

I heard a loud crunching noise. Who would be eating in the middle of a marsh?

"Well, iffen it ain't the fool boy what tosses stones."

"Who said that? Show yourself." I quickly turned, looking across the wetlands and saw no one. Taking a lower glance, I noted a woodchuck munching on what looked like an apple.

"Hey, ground hog, was it you who spoke?"

"Ya, betcha boy. It were me, and I'll tell you tain't smart ter mess with a wizard. I seed whatcha done. Wizard knows all yer tricks. He ain't much on hurtin us creatures."

"I only harmed you once, and not badly either. Why do you bother me?"

"Wall, ther young feller, I sees more of ya then them."

"Them? Who are them?"

"Them what thinks of ya only as a nuisance. I sees ya not jest as a fool boy, but the makings of a fine man one day."

"Oh, and what does the oracle of the ground hog see in my glorious future?"

"Listen here, ya damned whelp, thet attitude ain't gonna get yer anywheres. Thets what got yer in in trouble in the fust place. So shut yer yap and do whats I tell ya."

Am I delusional? Ground hogs can't speak. Can they? Well, they must cause, I'm talking to one right now. "All right, I can accept you can talk, but how do you know what I've done?"

He threw down the apple core and waddled closer to me. Looking like a little old fat man, he glared at me. Standing on his hind feet, he put his front paws on what I supposed were hips, pursing his lips, he continued scowling at me. As he stepped even closer, we were now nose to knee.

"Don't you get mad at me," I said.

"I didn't even want to come to the stinking palace. Wasn't anybody ever young? Everyone here is mad at me. Now a ground hog says I must do as he says. Why?"

"Yer, gots to realize, yer part of a group chosen by the Council of the Ancients. They run dad berned everythin. Now are ya gonna be smart and do whatcher told or be a dumb arse all yer life?"

Just then, a small falcon flew overhead. I reached down to grab a stone and he bit me. He bit me! And I'm bleeding.

Chapter 2

Merlin

I entered the king's quarters hoping to find Arthur in better form. But, alas such was not the case. He was growing thin, his eyes were dull and his skin as grey as a stone.

He didn't hear me enter so I, placed my hand on his shoulder and shook him.

"Merlin?" he whispered, "How fares my sister?"

I nodded, saying, "She feels the same as you."

Arthur shook his head. "All is lost then. The servants talk of death. Have many passed?" I did not wish to trouble him further.

"Not many, Sire, most all are ill, but not gravely so."

Arthur pushed himself up into a sitting position on his massive bed.

"Merlin, I sense you are holding something from me, old friend. What is it that you are not telling me?"

I hemmed and hawed, but I knew it not wise to withhold from the king.

"Sire, it is your sister. She is more ill than I have told you."

"Why would you not tell me the truth, Merlin? I know she and I were not always the best of friends, but we have reconciled. What is her true condition?"

"Arthur, she became ill before you and her symptoms are far worse. She has been vomiting for the past week and a half. I'm sorry I did not tell you sooner."

"Merlin, I am truly vexed with you. But, what's done is done. Was she the first to fall ill?"

"She was, Sire, as soon as she arrived from Avalon she was sick. I was certain no sickness was harbored on the mystic isle. But, how could she have contracted the illness between Avalon and the castle?"

This requires investigation. Is this some kind of conspiracy? Morganna has always had her enemies, but I doubt any would wish such a danger upon her. Who would so gravely endanger her? I must speak with Fiona. She has traveled the entire kingdom and may have something of import.

~ ~ ~

Chuck

"Well, lad are you ready to become a man?" *I wonder if this boy is even worthy. Can he withstand the test? Dad-berned councilers, they dun give me alla the hard ones. This feller gonna take a lotta work.*

"I'm awaitin, boy, What's it gonna be?"

This here boy needs to be frightened a bit. Dunt do it often, but I'll intimertate him with my size. I raised my front paw into the air and in an instant, I was a foot and a half taller than he.

The lad looked up at me as his eyes grew large with fear. I raised my paw agin and whoopee, now were nose to nose, as the lad has fallen to his knees.

"I will do as you bid, Sir Chuck."

The lad looked up at me as his eyes grew large with fear. I raised my paws agin, and whoopie, now wer nose to nose as the lad has fallen to the ground.

"Wall, lad, do yer think ya ken handle helpin another feller?"

Still too frightened to speak, he nodded. Pur boy he done lost his wits.

We was near the castle when I aspied Fiona. She was jest flyin in circles, not huntin, jest flyin, I lifted my paw in greetin, the lad faints. Fiona drops down ter see whats happin.

"Chuck, is this the boy who throws stones? What's the matter with him?"

"Ain't nuttin serious. He jest dropped cause he's ascared." Fiona moved to the lad's side.

Cockin her head sideways she says, "What has him so frightened?"

I chuckled. "Wall, yer probly don't knows it, but I ken be as big as a giant."

"A giant?" A confused look passed over her features.

"How can that be?"

"Well, jest yer rest them feathers, little gell. I needs ter tell ya sumpin."

"Chuck, what must you tell me? You're scaring me."

"Now don't yer fret gell tis nuttin to be afeared a. Jes tell me ya ever feel like the body yer in ain't the one ya started with?"

The pur little bird, she don't knows what ter make of all this.

"Chuck, yes I often feel I am in the wrong body. Neither do I fit in, with birds of my own species. Am I a misfit or just unable to be a part of any group?"

Gently, I lifted her onto a nearby rock and placed my front paws on her feets. She bowed her head an started ter cry.

"Fiona, why do yer weep? What I have ter tell yer ain't so bad. Honey gell, yer special, a chosen one."

"Chosen?"

She raised her head, then asked, "What am I chosen for?"

At that moment Finn woke up. "What's going on? You!" he said, pointin at me.

"What did you do to me? I demand answers." I raised my paws and agin he fainted.

~ ~ ~

Morganna

Damn, I can't understand why I'm so ill.

An authoritative knock at my door pulled me from my thoughts. It had to be Elaine. No one else knocks as if they were using a gavel.

"Come in, Elaine. What brings you here today?"

"Morganna, you must get well quickly. You are needed on the isle. Someone is following me, I can feel it."

"What is wrong? Some ritual you have forgotten how to perform? Why would anyone stalk you?"

Elaine shook with anger. She hated the fact that though she held the highest order, I had the greater knowledge of how to enact each ritual.

"No, Morganna, the problem is, each day more fall ill. Many have died. I need your help. I'm afraid the person who is tracking my every move is the cause for the sickness."

If I blame someone else, maybe I can save myself.

"Elaine, I truly would wish to assist you. Though I am somewhat better than I have been, it is impossible for me to leave this bed."

"But, Morganna, what am I to do? Everyone, everyone is sick. I can't handle everything by myself."

I rolled my eyes. The poor fool cannot handle anything, let alone everything.

"Elaine, find Merlin. He will tell you what must be done and by whom."

"What? Why?" Her eyes glazed over and she began to shake. She fell to the floor.

The woman is useless. There is no possibility I could help her. I'm just going to yell for someone, anyone.

Though the guards responded quickly, Merlin was present in an instant.

"Morganna," he said, "What is wrong? Why is Elaine on the floor?"

"I think it is part anger and part fear."

Merlin spoke. "Guards, pick her up and set her on the divan."

The guards did as they were bid and within moments she spoke. "What happened? Where am I?"

She glanced at me, and I knew within that moment, she was going to feign amnesia. Merlin being a fair-minded man was more concerned than suspicious.

"You are in Morganna's quarters. You fainted," the wizard kindly replied.

Elaine's lips opened in an enigmatic smile. I was certain she felt she duped the wizard.

This witch must be watched. There is no telling what further foulness she is capable of. What could her motives be? Could someone really be stalking her? If so, why? Who?

Merlin spoke up. "Morganna, I will take Elaine to my quarters and take care of her until she regains her memory."

I worried for the old man. Elaine's duplicity could well put him in grave danger.

~ ~ ~

Chuck

"Wall yer two gots a big job aheada ya." Though the boy was now conscious his face was dern near as puzzled as yer can get. His eyes are big as plates and his tongue is thick as a log. Pur feller cain't talk. Fiona, too wer flustered. *Sweet gell, but too nice fer her own self.*

I looked at the pair. I knew in my heart them two were the right critters. Cept Finn were still a lad. I guess I'll hafta do thisin by my ownself. Too late to call a Council meet.

"Nows, Fiona, a member yer told me ya didn't right fit in yer body?"

She hopped to the ground and stood afront a me dancing from one foot to the other.

"Listen ter me, little gell, you was chosen ter be a part of afixin this here sickness problem. Yer goona bees alright. Your weren't always a bird ya know. Yer jest set thar, whilst I make our friend Finn a critter jest like you."

I stood on me hind legs and raised my front paws high as I could. At once I grew very tall. I heard Finn whimper, but I couldn't stop now. Only gots one chance at this without councils say so's.

Repeating the words I'd larned so long ago, I prayed I done it keerect. I only done it three, maybe, four times afore. I looked down at Finn. He was a saken and his body was atakin some kinda new shape. But whatever he was twernt no bird. Dad bern it, he's a dang fox.

Now ter the best of my ameberin, foxes eats birds. Thisin isn't me best and I cain't do it over. The council would have me head, cause this ain't the fust time. I messed up, so I gots to figure a way fer them to gets along. Finn were a fine-lookin fox. Membe he's a mite smarter too. *Chuck yer made the mess. Now fix it.*

Fiona seein Finn as a fox flew to a high branch of a nearby tree. She were askart. Didn't blame her, she was often hunted by the red varmits.

"Wall, now we gots a problem."

The fox spoke up. "What do you mean 'we'? Looks to me like I am the only one with a problem. What are you going to do about it?" He grabbed my fur at my neck and shook me til my teeth rattled.

"I'ma guessin I gots ter larn yer two ta be friendly with each other."

Finn glared at me, fire in his eyes. Steppin toward me, growling, he was more than a mite scary.

"Hold on thar, fella, jest a little woops. Ain't much sense in eatin me. If ya do ya'll never be jest a boy again."

Finn stopped growling. He sat back on his haunches.

"Well, I guess I can't say nothing ever happens around here. I got no problem with the bird. It's kinda pretty."

"Good thinkin, boy. Now, Fiona, iffen we're gonna solve this sicken mess yer gots to get along. Kin you do thet?"

~ ~ ~

Merlin

I'd not seen Arthur in several days, so when I entered his quarters, I was astounded at his robust appearance.

"Arthur, I am so pleased to see you looking so well. What happened? Are you completely healed?" He rose from the bed and walked toward me.

"Well, I wouldn't say I'm fully healed but I owe my health to the little lady by the table."

I knew this lass, she was young, but efficient in her duties. I could not think of any reason she would harm the king.

"And how did she bring this about, Arthur?"

"She brought me the honey mead her mother makes. It is all I have been drinking and each day I feel more like myself."

This is quite strange. Could simple mead be the answer? I must meet with her mother. I looked to the corner of the room, where the maid had placed a covered container on the table.

"Arthur, what is the girl's name? I would like to speak with her mother. Is the woman a healer by any chance?"

"Not to my knowledge, Merlin, however she does make the finest mead I've ever tasted. Leona is the lass's name and her mother is called Harriet. Go with Leona, I do not need her further today."

"With your permission, Arthur, I shall." She looked up as she walked toward the door.

"Leona," I said, "Could I please walk with you to see your mother?"

"As you wish, Sire."

The lass was shy and soft spoken, so little was said until we reached a small cottage in the wood.

"Sire, is my mother in trouble?"

"Trouble? Why would you say that, lass?"

The girl looked down and mumbled, "No one has ever asked to see my mum before. I am certain she made the mead the same as always."

"Fear not, my child, your mother's mead may solve a dangerous situation. And please, Leona, please, understand neither you nor your mother is in danger of any sort. And you, young lady, may call me Merlin."

She looked up at me and smiled. A smile brighter than the sun itself.

~ ~ ~

Morganna

I feel a little better today, but I didn't feel I needed Elaine's company. She tires me out. So when I heard her distinctive knock I ignored it. But the knock became louder.

I shouted,

"Elaine, I'm resting, please, let me sleep." The knocking continued. "Elaine, please stop, you're giving me a headache."

"Morganna, it's me, Arthur."

"Come in, brother, you're always welcome. You're looking far better than Merlin told me."

"Yes, I am feeling much better. I think it's Harriet's honey mead. Merlin is trying to determine what ingredient is responsible for the healing."

I sat up in the bed, and Arthur plumped my pillows, making me far more comfortable.

"When you next see the wizard, would you please ask him to stop in and see me?"

"Of course, he is now on his way to talk to Harriet and he led me to believe he wishes to speak with you, when he returns. Morganna, Merlin said when you came from Avalon you were already sick. Is that true?"

"Yes, but I got only slightly better staying here."

"Why," he asked, "What is the same here as there, but different somehow?" I was growing tired, as I had finished the apple and cheese that was my lunch. My eyes were beginning to droop. "Arthur, I don't wish to be rude, but I am suddenly feeling extremely tired. Please excuse me."

"Of course, I have no wish to disturb the sleep you so sorely need. Rest well and I will tell Merlin not to bother you until dinner."

"Thank you."

~ ~ ~

Merlin

'Twas not far from the small town outside of the castle to the wood where Leona and her mother lived.

Leona knocked, called to her mother, and pushed open the door. The cottage was small and very well kept. Unusual for peasant cottages, the walls were covered with beautiful drawings of flowers and herbs. Each rendered beautifully and very accurate. Harriet was startled but not frightened.

"Leona, do you know who you have brought to our humble home?"

"Yes, Mum, he's a wizard."

"Child, he's not *a* wizard, he's *the* wizard. Merlin, the greatest wizard of all." I blushed. Though true, it was a heartfelt compliment.

"Come, come," Harriet said, directing me to a long table. At one end was a large flat stone, that looked to be marble.

"Thank you," I said as I marveled at the decorated walls and the stone floor.

"Harriet, your home is a wonder. I've never seen a more beautiful cottage. It's fit for royalty. Did you paint the walls yourself?"

"Thank you. Not alone. Each mead maker must learn the items that go into the mead. Leona has helped once she was old enough to draw. It must be clean else the mead would not taste as sweet. Would you like some?"

"Indeed, that is in part the reason I've come. The King tells me it is the finest he's ever tasted."

The ample woman grew red in the face and giggled. "Oh my, that is such an honor. Please do tell him I thank him very much."

"I shall do so, madam. Now, will you tell me exactly how you make this wonderous mead?"

"I'm so sorry, Master Merlin, tis a secret. The recipe has been handed down in my family for generations. Each of us must swear not to tell a soul outside of the family. It is an oath that can't be broken."

"I understand, my good woman, however your mead has played a critical role in healing the king of a very strange illness."

"Please, Master Merlin, I cannot reveal the recipe. I cannot break my sacred oath."

"I understand, Harriet, but at this moment, you could well be the savior of an entire kingdom."

The poor woman was crying. Tears sprang to her eyes as she bit her lower lip. I know well her frustration. She was a good woman whose word was well respected.

I'm sure she feels her soul would be lost if she reveals the secret of the mead, but there is too much at stake.

"Madam, is there an elder of your family who lives nearby?"

Harriet grew quiet. She tapped her finger against her lips, then her eyes lit up.

"Yes, Master Merlin, my father. He doesn't live here, but he is visiting. Leona, please fetch Grandpa. He's at the Laughing Duck Pub. Hurry girl."

I could feel her relief, it was palpable. Now it was left to me to obtain the old gentleman's consent. The pub must be nearby as Leona and the grandfather returned rather quickly. The man was quite spry for his years. I was certain Leona had told him of our predicament and I expected the man to reject my plea. However, he smiled and extended his hand.

"Hello, Master Merlin. Leona tells me you have a grave situation. How can I help?"

"You know who I am but I don't believe I've ever met you. What is your name?"

The old man smiled broadly and said, "Family calls me Gramps. Friends use me given name, Shawn. Now what's the problem, Wizard?"

Chapter 3

Chuck

Wall, I can sees whose gonna win this here race. lad's got a mean streak, but I think his competition sense, will keep him out of trouble and on his toes. He ain't a bad looken fox, but there is the problem foxes and falcons aren't usually on friendly terms.

"Fiona, can you make sure you're out of his way till he understands he's part of a team?"

"Sure, Chuck, somehow I don't think it will take long. He is kinda cute."

"Now how does cute make him part of a team on a mission?"

"Hey, wait a minute, first you turn me into a fox, now I'm on a mission. Oh, Chuck, just so you know I won't eat her. Told ya she's pretty and she thinks I'm cute."

"Never mind all this romatical stuff, you have a very important task to undertake. Now gets serous."

The bird flew from her perch in the tree to the log where Finn sat. He turned his head and looked directly at the bird.

"Well, Fiona, can we work together? I promise not to eat you."

~ ~ ~

Merlin

Shawn told me he would give me his decision by the end of the week. He will confer with other elders in his family and send his answer as soon as the conclusion is reached. Which I felt was more than fair.

Leona and I were heading back to the castle when I saw Chuck near the marsh. The groundhog stood and waved. It was a strange kind of wave, almost as if he wanted me to join him.

"Leona, go on ahead. I'll be there momentarily."

Leona nodded and continued to the castle. As I grew close to the marsh, I saw Chuck was not alone. Finn and Fiona were with him. Both sitting quietly on a log.

"Chuck," I said," how are you? Is something amiss?"

"Not really, Merlin, I jest kinda concerned bout Finn and Fiona aworken together. They says they can do it, but I dinno falcons and foxes, I dinno."

"My good man, think. Neither are as they appear. They can and will work together."

I raised my hand to the sky. A book appeared, and I snatched it from the air.

"Wow, Master Merlin, thet thar is some trick," Chuck commented. "It is not a trick. It is, in fact, magic."

"Pose thet makes sense. Considern."

"That it does, my friend. This book contains the instructions you will need to direct these youngsters in their most important endeavor." Chuck raised up on his haunches and saluted me. Certain Chuck could do all that was required, I continued to the castle. Leona would be waiting. I went straight to my quarters, but she was not there. As reliable as she is in her duties, she probably returned to her appointed tasks.

I found the chatelaine and asked if she knew of Leona's whereabouts. "Certainly. Master Merlin, she was in the great hall. His Highness came in and asked for her to come with him. I don't know where they went, sire."

I headed for Arthur's chambers. As his quarters were just after of those of his sister, I noted her door was open. I heard Morganna speaking to the king.

"I'm glad you are feeling much better, brother. I am not yet strong enough to leave my bed."

"I understand, but you must aid me."

I knocked gently and entered. "Your Highness, Morganna, I don't mean to intrude, however I overheard you."

"Quite understandable," Arthur said.

"We were discussing the strange illness that has befallen us."

~ ~ ~

Elaine

This is actually working out better than I planned. I thought poisoning the sacred well would only affect the dwellers of Avalon. Yet somehow the waters reach the Camelot well also.

I must do something to ease the spread of the sickness. Too many have died, but I know not how to remove the poison. I must contact Morganna.

Confiding in her would be foolhardy. So, I will ask her about the link between Avalon and Camelot. Somehow, I will need to be the hero in solving the problem rather than the perpetrator. I'm convinced it's my stalker. I did not put in a huge amount of poison. Only those on the isle should be affected and none should die, only sickened.

Carefully, I dressed in very subdued outfit and wore none of my jewels I usually wear. I will present myself as a demur, concerned priestess. Alone, I summoned the boatmen and went ashore to speak to Morganna. Though it was quite a walk from the shore, I did not want an escort, nor even a horse. The walk would tire me and increase my concerned look. However, my ankle pain was greatly eased.

As I neared the castle, I noted an unusual sight at the edge of the marsh. A ground hog stood erect in his hind legs. He appeared to be directing or teaching a fox and a falcon.

Do I see this or is it an apparition? I'm beginning to doubt. Perhaps I should leave? This may not be the best action for me to take. I think I shall return and think on this more diligently.

Turning before I thought could be seen, Merlin however did see me. He called to me as he walked over the moat bridge. I stepped into the damp grass at the edge of the moat, so my ankle could be in the cool weeds.

"Elaine, I would like to speak with you."

"Hello, Master Merlin, but I have pressing duties on the isle. Please forgive me."

"Those matters will wait for a bit. I assure you the matters of Camelot are *far more pressing.*" He walked toward me. I did not dare thwart him. Standing as erect as possible, I pulled my shawl up over my shoulders and placed the cloth over my head. Merlin is very intuitive and might easily discern my true motive. It is hard to fool a wizard.

I stepped toward him showing my timid demeanor. "What do you wish to speak about, Merlin?"

"I should think that would be obvious. The sickness that has stricken most of the kingdom. Do not think to play the fool with me, Elaine. What have you learned?"

"Learned? Nothing. I've just come to ask Morganna if she has any insight?"

The wizard glared at me. *Could he know I am the culprit?*

~ ~ ~

Finn

"Hey, Master Chuck, why is Merlin shaking his finger at Lady Elaine? Looks like he's mad, real mad."

"Master Chuck? Oh, I like thet." The ground hog seemed more interested that I'd given him a title than the fact, that Merlin is madder than a wet hen.

"Hey, Finn yer right, he's really mad. I neva seed him this angry. Maybe we should find out jest whats gonn on."

"Fiona," I hollored,

"Come on we have to see what is happening." She flew ahead of me as I raced along the edge of the marsh.

The wood chuck stood on his haunches and shouted, "Ya dad berned critters. I be lucky iffen I ever gets a new assignment, iffen yer kills each other."

I called to Fiona, "You go to the castle and learn what you can from Merlin. I'll foller Elaine."

As I got closer, I could hear her sobbing and wondered why. Merlin was very upset, but he would never harm a woman. She cried so deeply she could not see. She faulted in her step and fell to the ground. She screamed as if she was hit by an arrow. I lowered myself into the tall grasses and crept forward.

Again, she was crying and holding her ankle, which seemed to grow larger as I watched. She tried to stand and fell as soon as she put weight on her injured foot.

I knew I couldn't help her. So, I raced back to Chuck. He'd know how to aid her. When I approached the marsh, Chuck saw me and indicated I was to join him and Fiona.

"Hi, Chuck, Fiona. Elaine has fallen and hurt her ankle. She needs help."

"Thet gal is shore a mess. Fiona, fly and get Merlin. He'll fix everthin. Did she tell ya anythin?"

"She didn't talk at all. Just crying and sobbing. She wouldn't have fallen if her eyes weren't full of tears."

"Wall, I guess seems like fallen woulda be enuf ter make her cry."

"Yes, it would, but she was crying before she fell. She started sobbing when Merlin turned away from her."

The woodchuck nodded, saying, "I pose then, he'll know why she was aweeping."

I looked at him skeptically, this whole mess is as confusing as it could possibly be.

I called to Fiona, "You go to the castle and learn what you can from Merlin. I'll tail Elaine."

She raised one wing in assent. I raced to catch up with the priestess.

Chapter 4

King Arthur

I am amazed how much better I feel for having ingested only Harriet's mead. I wonder how Morganna fares.

As I stepped from my quarters, I heard a sweet humming. The closer I came to Morganna's rooms the louder the sound became.

Her door was ajar. I pushed it open and cleared my throat so I wouldn't startle her. I looked at the bed. She was not there. The humming stopped. I turned and saw her sitting by the window.

"Arthur, it's so nice to see you. It seems ages ago we were both ill."

"It does. Merlin told me you could not leave your bed and now I find you sitting in a chair and humming. It's amazing."

"Well, brother, I decided to take your advice."

"My advice? What do you mean?"

"For the last week I've only drank Harriet's mead. It is as if she is a sorceress."

"Now, Morganna, do not start foolish rumors. This woman is a marvelous mead maker, follows her vows and reveres her family. Please simply honor the one who has given of her healing brew."

"Relax, brother, I speak in jest, for your ears only."

"Be certain, sister, for such a rumor would only compound our present problem."

"Fear not, Arthur, I am neither foolish nor uncaring. Remember my people are afflicted as well."

I nodded, and we continued our discussion and shared what each of us had deduced. A gentle knock sounded at Morganna's door.

"Excuse me, folks, may I enter?"

Morganna replied, "Of course, Merlin, you are always welcome."

"I've been speaking to Chuck."

"Chuck? Who's Chuck?" she asked.

"Just an old friend. He's asked if I have drawings of the castle's interior," the sorcerer answered.

"Of course, we have all the drawings. They are in the heraldry room. I don't think though that anyone has seen them since the castle was completed, before Uther's time. I've added much and those drawings are there as well." I was pleased that I'd kept all the castle's renderings. Some told me I was foolish to do so, but somehow, I knew better," Arthur stated.

The old wizard rubbed his hands together, saying, "Good, good, Arthur, we now have the beginnings of a plan."

"Merlin, do you want me to deliver them to your quarters or to the war room?"

"The war room has a larger table. I'm bringing some others with me, and the bigger table will make the plan more clear to all." The old man began to pace back and forth all the while pulling on his long white beard.

Gently I placed my hand on the wizard's shoulder. "Yes, yes what?" he stammered.

"Calm yourself, man, we'll figure this out. I'll speak to Morganna, and she will consult Elaine. We'll meet here tomorrow at first light."

"Good, good, excellent. That is wise, Arthur. With the early hour there will be fewer around. It would not do if everyone knows of our plans. Rumors travel fast and if there is a certain culprit, it would warn him of our knowledge."

"Quite so, old friend. I'll see Morganna at once and request that she contact Elaine."

~ ~ ~

Finn

I followed Elaine as close as I dared. Ahead was an open meadow. Not wanting her to see me, I pressed my body close to the earth. It was then I realized even if she does see me, it won't matter. I'd forgotten I am a fox. Creatures often found in meadows.

The terrain was somewhat unusual. Camelot, though built on a hill above the sea, was far below the spirals of the Glastonbury Monastery. Suddenly the area all around me filled with a thick fog, so dense I realized I was lost. I tried stepping directly into the mist, but the thickness remained. Casually I stepped further into the most concentrated part of the misty cloud, that even obscured the sunlight. I was more frightened than I'd ever been. It seemed so solid I tried to push it out of the way, my paw disappeared. A mere leg's length away, yet I could not see it.

A faint humming pierced the fog. I recognized the sound as being Elaine's, as I'd heard her hum once before. At once the mist lifted and I saw her standing in the middle of a boat, her hands uplifted. She kept looking all around her, as if she were being watched. As she lowered them, I saw her no more. *How can I follow what I cannot see?*

Chapter 5

Fiona

Of course, I'd flown over the misted Isle before, but I've never seen the mist so dense. As if Avalon is hiding herself.

I circled around and at the very edge of the fog, was a spot of red. Could it be? Gliding closed to the ground, I noted it was, in fact, Finn. Pushing my feet forward I landed gently beside him. The mist seemed to creep from him over to the lakeshore. We were unable to see Avalon.

"Hello, Finn," I said, as I felt my heart hammer against my chest. "Fiona, something tells me there is more than one way into Avalon."

"You're right, but it isn't easy. Especially if you can't fly."

"I know, Miss Falcon, you don't need to remind me."

"Sorry, Finn, I didn't mean to tease you. Look, Elaine is going up to the monastery."

"I guess her ankle is not as painful as I first believed. But why would a Goddess of Avalon seek out a Catholic monastery?"

"I don't know. Maybe she seeks redemption for her sins."

Finn nodded, saying, "Well, we are supposed to follow her, so let's go."

I watched as the fox chose the most difficult path for himself. "Wait, Finn, let me see if I can find a more direct route. The way you are going will take too long." I flew straight up, knowing Finn would not take the impossible path. All around the tor I flew. I noticed a little used but easy route to the top. I guess monks were like goddesses in that neither would take the easy way. Apparently, the path was only used by small animals. If only he doesn't come across a small rabbit, we'll make it. I shouted down to Finn, "Follow me, I've found a quicker way."

In short order we ascended the tor. Elaine was only a few paces ahead. She entered the Church proper and seeing a monk, she inquired, "Sire, what do I have to do to make a confession?"

"Quite simple, my lady. You see those cabinets over there?" he said, pointing to the far wall. "That is the confessional."

"You mean I go in and all my sins will be washed away?"

The monk smiled and gently eased her to one of the benches on either side of the aisle. "Sit here, my lady, and I shall find a priest. He will help you."

I flew up to the rafters and Finn crept underneath the bench she sat on. The priest approached and Finn scuttled into the nearest set of cabinets.

The priest leaned over Elaine and spoke to her softly. I could not hear what he was saying. They went on to adjoining cabinets. Though the priest spoke softly, I could not understand. Elaine began to cry. I waited until she became calm, and her speech became more intelligible.

"Father, I'm so afraid. I think a man follows me and has done something to the water supply to make people very sick. Some have died."

"That is very serious, my child. Do you know who tracks your movements?"

"No, Father, I've had this feeling since my wedding day." I flew away. Merlin must know of this at once.

Chapter 6

Morganna

As there were only two of us in the war room, our voices reverberated against the walls. It sounded as if we were shouting. We were not, but each of us lowered our voices to a whisper.

"I thought Merlin and Elaine were to meet us here."

"I don't know where Elaine is, but Merlin sent word he is giving some instruction to Finn and Fiona," Arthur answered.

"Understandable. I see he sent us the drawings," I replied.

He laid them out, placing weights at the corners. I ran my hand over the vellum. It had the curve from being rolled together, yet if it were the original, it would be yellowed and crinkled.

"Arthur these can't be the originals. They are not that old."

"No, not the first made, I only asked for the most recent. Why would you want to see the originals?"

"Because, Arthur, they will show the land and the courses of waters, the sea and the lakes, not the castle's improvements."

"So, you don't think the problem is within either Avalon or Camelot?"

"That's right, brother, and we got well when we stopped drinking the water. Right?"

"Yes, but was it not Harriet's mead that cured us?"

"Sometimes, you are as foolish as a novice on her first day."

"Well let's be certain of the cause and the cure," Arthur replied.

~ ~ ~

Merlin

After speaking with Chuck, I quickly realized he had no need of my instruction. He sent out his charges with all they needed to know. I was unable to find Elaine, but the ground hog had Finn and Fiona following her. As I headed toward Camelot, I noticed a gentleman waving at me. As I grew closer, I recognized it was Harriet's father.

"Hello there, Shawn. What brings you to Camelot today?"

"Well, Merlin, my friend, I've come to see if my daughter's mead is the single answer you require?"

"I wish it were the final answer, but we need to find the cause as well as the cure."

"Certainly, makes sense. If you don't know the cause soon, the body would require stronger and stronger cures. Is there anything I can do to help?"

"Hopefully, my friend, you can. Were any of your elders here when Camelot was first built?"

"Aye, old Ethan is still about. He has many years but was just a boy when the castle was built."

"Do you think he would recall anything of the builders or their renderings?"

"Perhaps. I'm told he was a curious lad and had his nose in everything about that castle."

"Would you mind speaking with him?"

"Of course not, Merlin. I'll send any information by my fastest messenger."

"Thank you, Shawn." I watched the old man as he walked toward his village. It is a relief to have assistance in this matter. I turned and headed to the marsh near the castle.

Chuck saw me and waddled toward me. "Ah, Merlin, have ya a moment? I needs ter tell yer whats happened."

"Go on then, I'm late for a meeting with Morganna, Arthur, and Elaine."

"Elaine will not be comin. Fiona has jes flown in ter tell me her and Finn follered Elaine ter the monastery at Glastonbury."

"Glastonbury? Why? Elaine is a High Priestess of Avalon, why would she go there?"

"Don't know, but Fiona is going back to see if Finn has the answer?" Chuck replied.

"All right then, seems you have everything under control. I must speak with Morganna and Arthur. If there is any new information, I'll send a messenger at once."

Chapter 7

Breasal (man who follows Elaine)

I will have that perfect woman if it is the last thing I do. Since I first beheld her, I knew she was the one, the only one, for me.

After years of seeking, I finally followed her closer than I had dared before. It was my belief her trail would lead to the so-called Misted Isle. Always I lost her as the fog lifted then fell as quickly as it rose, and I could see her no more. This time she took a slightly different route and no mist clouded my vision.

I first saw her on her wedding day. She was beautiful, but why was she marrying that massive idiot? I could treat far better far better than he. He is just big. Nothing else about him is impressive.

I have great wealth, we could travel the world. Anywhere and everywhere, she wanted to go. Why? Why does she spurn me?

However, the biggest question of all is why did she go to a monastery? I've always known she was of Avalon. Why the drastic change of beliefs? I will have her, even if it means killing the king himself.

~ ~ ~

Finn

Elaine went in the main door. I will go around to the side. As I did so, I saw the window is opened a crack, maybe I can hear her and whoever she is with. Their voices are faint, but I can hear her clearly. I stayed on the side of the monastery until Elaine took her leave. She did not return to the shore where she arrived. Apparently, she knew another way. Going to the back of the building, she hiked up her skirt to avoid getting it wet, on the dew-soaked grass. She went down a very narrow path. It was not a well-used path but clearly a route to somewhere. I've often seen small animals leave a distinctive trail, yet one that predators can't easily find.

I followed the path, as it led past the famed Avalon, it was beautiful beyond description. and ended near a village I'd never seen before. The people seemed to be of small stature. Though they did not seem hostile, I remembered someone told me the boatmen for Avalon were of small height. Everything in the town was diminutive. I never knew such people existed. Does Fiona know of these folks? She probably does. She is the most intelligent being I've ever met, to say nothing of her beauty. I know I will become a man again if I bring this mystery to a close, but I wish Fiona could be a woman, my woman.

I knew Fiona would return to the castle rookery, so I too continued to Camelot as well. As I neared the castle, I noted Chuck standing on his haunches, waving his front paws.

"Hey thar, Finn, whar ya going? Ya seed Fiona? She were supposed ter report ter me, yet I ain't seed her in dang near two days."

"She's gone back to the rookery. I'm headed there too. I'll tell her you are looking for her."

"Thanks, Finn, I'll see ya later," the ground hog replied, as he went from a standing position to a scamper deeper into the swamp.

I was tired, so I sat back on my haunches, just to rest a bit before I went in the castle. I was daydreaming about how good our lives could be if only we were both human, that I paid no attention to my surroundings. Suddenly, everything went dark. Some kind of heavy cloth was over my head and I felt a vise grip on my body. I don't know who or why anyone would have cause to kidnap me. Whoever it was tied the cloth bag around my neck, I suppose to create fear. I shall not give satisfaction.

Whoever it was, was speaking to me. I do not recognize the voice, so I'll not speak, but I shall fight whoever has laid hands upon me, kicking until I actually hit the being who captured me.

"Well little one, for some reason I do not believe you are a simple woodland fox. I don't understand, but something tells me you know my beloved. Elaine. You might as well settle down. You *will* lead me to my Elaine." I struck out again, this time making more of an effort, as whoever it was, cried out in pain. My rear claw found skin and I pressed my paw as hard as I could. I heard him shriek as he dropped me to the floor. Apparently, I'd drawn blood, as he shook his hand and blood spattered everywhere.

I wonder how he came to connect me with the Priestess of Avalon? Perhaps he thought me to be her pet. And why would Elaine be his beloved? She's married. I can't imagine a priestess violating marriage vows. I know she isn't overly fond of her husband, but I'd never seen her with another man.

Where is this fool taking me? He's carried me for what seemed like hours, until I heard the sound of the surf. Camelot was some distance from the sea. Kicking the one that held me seemed to be the only way I could retaliate. My back legs went out but connected to nothing. He set me on the ground. I wanted to run, but since I can't see I might run into something. I sat down and he reached under the covering and tied a rope about my neck, then removed the sack. He is a man I do not recognize. Who is he and what did he want with me? I had little time to formulate a plan, as I was thrown into a metal cage of some kind.

There was no possible way he could know I am not simple a woodland creature. I look like every other fox.

~ ~ ~

Fiona

I flew back to the castle. Before I went to the rookery, I sought Merlin. He wasn't in his quarters. So, I headed for the war room and overheard Merlin and the King conferring. The door was ajar. I knocked with my beak and flew in.

"Ah, Fiona, have you learned something?" Merlin inquired.

"I have, Sire, but I do not know if it is connected to the illness problem."

"Well, girl, please tell us what you discovered," the King said.

"When we first followed Elaine, she didn't go to Avalon, so we continued. Merlin, she went to the monastery."

Surprised by my information, the mage pushed back his seat at the round table and stood. I swear the man grew seven feet. He clenched his jaw, and his eyes seemed to grow dark with anger.

"Why? Are you certain? Glastonbury is not that far from Avalon," the King interjected.

"Sire, I do not know why she went there, but Finn and I listened to her confession. She talked to a priest."

"A priest? But why?" the King interjected.

"Your Highness, I do not know." I walked on the table to be closer to the men. "Finn told me to come here and tell you what we learned, as soon as possible. He said he would follow her and meet me here."

The King went silent and turned his back to us. I asked Merlin what he would have me do. He too turned, his beard snapping as he moved. He spoke no more,

What am I to do? Finn is missing, the King and Merlin aren't speaking. I will seek out Morganna. Now that she is well, she might have returned to Avalon. *I sure hope not.*

Though I've flown over it many times, I do not believe I could penetrate the Mists of Avalon.

Hurrying through the Camelot corridors, I found Morganna in the quarters that Arthur always had ready for her. She was packing. The wardrobe was now empty. Her raiment tucked away in a large trunk.

"Morganna, are you leaving?"

"Yes, my little falcon, I must return to my duties on the isle. Elaine seems somehow lost within herself. She's done none of her tasks since I became ill. She used to report to me daily, so I could instruct her, yet I've not seen her in three days. Has something happened to her?"

"She is not harmed physically, but just today she went to Glastonbury. Morganna, she had her confession heard."

"What? Confession? In a church?"

"Yes, Morganna, In the monastery at Glastonbury."

"Fiona, does Merlin know?"

"Yes, I told both him and King Arthur. When I did, they both turned their backs and not another word was spoken. Do you know why, my lady? Have I done something wrong?"

"Well, I can't very well leave now. Not if Elaine is insane." She turned from me and asked her maid to unpack what she had just packed.

"I know it sounds silly, but please, Marie, I'll explain later." She grabbed a cloak and hurried out the door.

She indicated I was to accompany her. Though as a rule, flight is much faster than most people can run, I found it difficult to keep up with the priestess. We reached the lake whereon Avalon and the monastery were built. Morganna raised her hands over her head and touched them palm to palm. Then slowly turning her palms down, she lowered them to her sides. As her hands touched her body, the mist lowered, and a small dark man approached in a flat-bottomed boat. He pulled the boat to shore and stood to make it easier for the priestess to enter. I flew to her shoulder and perched there, as she stood in the prow of the boat and did not sit down. The man dipped the oars into the water soundlessly, and the mist rose again behind us. I was awestruck. The silence was so profound it was hard to grasp. Nothing made a sound, not birds, nor breeze. I'd never known such a lack of sound.

When we reached the opposite shore Morganna stepped regally out of the boat. I rode on her shoulder. Looking up at the magnificent structure snuggled into the hill I was once again astounded by the beauty that was before me.

~ ~ ~

Finn

Why does this fool think there is some connection between the Avalon Priestess and me?

"There is no question, little fox. I sense you are known to my Elaine. For you see, I am not simply a man. I am the greatest mage who ever lived. Greater even the fabled Merlin."

I could remain silent no longer. "There is a reason, he is known throughout the land. His skills exceed yours. And I've never even heard of you. Who are you?"

"You shall be most surprised when you learn my name little fox. For though it is known among the major mages, perhaps, it does not reach the ears of woodland creatures, however the creatures may be enchanted."

He was truly a fool but apparently, a fool with skills. How does he know I am not actually a fox? This being is not as simple man as I supposed, he has the air of mage about him.

"Yes, my furry friend, I am Breasal the Bold."

Strange, that name is one I recall from some of Merlin's lengthy instructions.

"Your name is one I have heard before. Though I believe Merlin addresses you as Breasal the Weasel."

He stood, his arms extended as if he were singing. When he heard my taunt, he spun around, screaming, "That is not true! Even the Merlin knows, I am Breasal the Bold."

"No, the Merlin is never wrong, nor does he lie. You are the weasel who was banished for his foul machinations. It is said only the High Priestess of Avalon can redeem him."

Chapter 8

My flight was tiring, and now I feel bereft, something is missing. Finn is in trouble. I can feel it in my heart. *Should I tell the others, or will they think I am addled-brained?*

The Merlin sat at the round table, his head in his hands. His shoulders sank as he sighed. I flew to him and sat upon his shoulder.

"What troubles you so, Merlin?"

"It's rather difficult to explain, Fiona. I feel as if someone is in danger."

"Yes, yes, I feel it too. Finn has not returned. Something must have happened to him. We must find him."

"He has not been in the rookery? How long has he been gone? Did you check the war room? Perhaps, he is looking for us. Arthur and I told him we would be there as soon as he returned. I realize we were harsh with you, for that I'm sorry."

"It doesn't matter. What is of most importance now is finding Finn. I should have stayed with him."

"This is not your fault, Fiona. He is a grown man, well, grown fox. Do you know if he has any friends?"

"Only Chuck, that I know of. Being a fox who is really a man, is kind of hard to explain to your friends. I told Morganna before I found you. She was leaving, but she stopped her packing and left. It was as if she knew exactly where to find him."

"Fiona do you think you can fly over Avalon and see Morganna and Elaine?"

"But, Master Merlin, I cannot penetrate the mist alone."

"You went in with Morganna, did you not?"

"Well, yes but…"

"No buts, you can go with me." He pointed to his shoulder and I flew and landed upon it. The mage walked rapidly and within moments we were at the lake shore. Merlin whistled and the same small man appeared. The man looked up and upon seeing the mage he froze momentarily, then quietly slipped the oar into the water. As he drew the boat onto the shore he bowed to Merlin and bid us enter.

Merlin is an old man so I thought he would rest and sit in the boat. He did not. As Morganna had, he stood and raised his staff toward the sky. The mist descended and Merlin sank down onto the seat of the boat. As before, the fog rose. We saw Avalon appear before us as the haze descended at our backs.

Morganna raced to us and enfolded Merlin in her arms. I flew up to a nearby tree.

"Merlin, Elaine has not been seen in several days. She told her maid she would see her in a while but did not say where she was going."

"Have you used your searching powers?"

I looked at the confused features on face of Morganna. Turning rapidly, she grabbed Merlin by the shoulders. She held him tightly, as he tried to pry her fingers from his person.

"Good gracious, woman what is wrong?" the mage cried out.

She dropped her hands, saying, "I am sorry, Merlin, I have been so long on Avalon, I forget I have that skill."

"Well, you do," he replied, shaking himself.

I flew down from the tree landing on her shoulder. "Can I help?" I have been a bird for as long as I remember. I performed only the observations to Morganna and the mage. "Please, Morganna, let me help more than I have been able to so far. I know Finn is not really a fox, do I have another identity as well?"

Morganna turned to face Merlin, saying, "Oh, my stars, she's right, I'd known her for so long I 'd forgotten she and Finn, have similar powers. It's been centuries since she was transformed. She may remember some incidents, but I am certain she does not recall the whole of it."

Merlin looked as confused as Morganna had been. He shook his head, causing his long white beard to sway. I wasn't sure how I could assist, but feel another species might be more helpful, if I could be on the ground on four legs instead of my two skinny ones. Flight is joyous, but after so many long years as a bird, I long to be a land creature, my feet walking on the ground.

The sorcerer stopped shaking his head and beard. I am certain he'd forgotten as well. "Morganna, we are a pair of idiots. I guess it has been so peaceful and problem free, when a problem does appear, we forget our skills."

"Merlin, Breasel has only known Fiona, as a bird. If she were a woman, we could have her pretend to be a higher-ranking priestess that Elaine. The man is a fool, he does not love Elaine, he just wants a priestess of Avalon, who can rid him of his transgressions."

I looked at them, outraged, "You mean I do have another identity? Why did you not tell me? Merlin, I've always done as you bid, why would you keep me in this from me, if I am actually a human woman? You said 'woman' so I assume I am a human. Why, why would you keep this from me?"

Merlin looked thoughtful, as if he saw what might happen. I tried to get him to give me an answer. He would not even look at me. I flew at him, though he would not look at me, he turned and swung his arms at me. Well, at least he knows I'm not happy.

Morganna saw I was agitated and becoming more so with each passing minute. She touched his arm and he seemed to come out of a trance of some sort. He then stared at me, as if he did not recognize me. It made me angry. I fluffed my feathers making myself as large as possible and flew to his shoulder making as much noise as I could. He covered his ears and pulled his head to his chest, forcing me to leave his shoulder.

Morganna touched his arm again, and he flew into a temper, the like of which I had never seen in all the years I have known him.

She yelled at such a high pitch my ears rang. "Merlin, you know as well as I, the spell for reanimation of a changeling before its time is dangerous. Extremely dangerous. I personally know not a single person who has used the incantation with positive results."

"Yes," he replied, speaking through his teeth, "but you know I am far older than you. I have not only seen the spell used to success. I, myself, have performed it many times with great positivity. Fear not, Morganna, I shall allow nothing to stand in the way of the completion of this mission. Too many lives are at stake." He seemed to be calm once again.

I was past anger. "Why? Why? Have you kept this from me? I've aided in every possible manner." I flew at their faces. I know it's wrong, but I don't have another option. Pay attention. They finally noticed me up in the tree above them. "It's been so long, I vaguely remember being a lass. You owe me at the very least an explanation."

The sorcerer shook his head. "Yes, Fiona, we do owe you that and a great deal more. What you have done for the world low these many centuries are far more that I can ever repay."

I was dumbfounded. I did not realize I'd been in his service that long. "The past is past, Merlin. Let's deal with the present. Why was I not told I could be a woman again? I assume, I was one a long time ago?"

Morganna walked beneath the tree and lifted her arm to me. "Come down, Fiona. We have another task for you. It may be difficult, but you are very skilled, else we would not designate such a task to you. You must know Merlin and I are very proud of the work you've done."

"I understand, Morganna. I hold no grudges for the past, but if you wish my further cooperation, you will not withhold anything from me."

Chapter 9

Bresal

I saw the fox waken from the blow I'd dealt him. He is now in the metal cage where he shall remain, until I can turn the priestess to my way of thinking.

After I hid the fox's cage under a pile of dead leaves I found in the cave, I went to see the High Priestess of Avalon. I'd given her a mild sedative that I might take her to the cave.

I placed her in a royal suite with every amenity I could think of. It is still a cave, however I did everything I could, that she might believe she is in the finest of accommodations. She must be treated well in order to earn her compliance. I've created this haven for her.

"Who are you?" she asked, speaking groggily. Bowing ever so slightly I replied, "I am the one who has admired you for many years. I am known as Breasel the Bold."

She looked at me as if trying to recognize me. Over the years I've spent watching her, she never noticed me. Her eyelids grew heavy, and she fell back onto the bed. She would not remember the surroundings.

Though somewhat disheveled, she was the loveliest creature I ever saw. However, it is not her beauty that draws me to her. What I desire, more than riches, more than prestige, is the power. The power to wipe away any misdoings. I want to be a greater sorcerer than the all-powerful Merlin. Once my transgressions are wiped from my soul, I can obtain the grimoire that only the purest of mages can touch.

This cave is too obvious. Someone might find her. I need a better hiding place. Though I searched for many days and had determined this was the best to be found, it will not do. Elaine required the finest of accommodations. I walked past the cemetery behind the chapel and found an overgrown path. There is a large mausoleum, well-hidden and seldom even seen. *Breasal, you are a genius.* It was placed deep in the woods, probably the tombs of royalty. The building was covered in thick, dense Ivy, it appeared that no one had entered in many years.

I cut a small hole where I assumed the opening was, as a building of this size usually has a large key on the shortest side of the structure. Pulling aside enough ivy that I could see more, I found a lock with a rusted key hanging in it. When I touched it, the key crumbled in my fingers. I was astounded. A light emanated from the keyhole and the door sprung open.

I held the fox in the cage. As I set the fox down, I noted a much larger room. It was a room fit for a queen. Not a burial tomb, but quarters for a living queen. While the room I'd prepared in the cave was luxurious, it pales in comparison to this. If I retrieve Elaine and give her this marvel, she will be grateful and give me the sacred grimoire.

I hastened to the cave and removed the spell I'd placed on the entrance. The ground around the mausoleum was unusually soft. It was almost like a bog. I stepped carefully, as I returned to the chamber. Once inside I found her in a deep slumber on the large bed. Gently I picked her up, being careful not to awaken her. Thankfully, the cave was only a short distance from the mausoleum and Elaine though quite tall, was not heavy. Unlocking the spell, I put on the cave, I carried her outside and headed on to the mausoleum and carefully placed her on the bed. Truly this was made for the most esteemed of the royals. The King perhaps? It was covered in soft furs and the pillows were made of finest silk. It was the most beautiful room I ever saw.

~ ~ ~

Finn

How do I get myself out of this mess? He's placed me in the damn cave now I find myself in some kind of crypt. That pompous ass Breasal left the door open. Peering through the opening I could see part of a graveyard. I turned from the outside view and saw a large room at the back of this tomb. The High Priestess of Avalon was laid out on the large bed like a bride. It was clear she had been drugged. Why does he want us? I have no connection to Elaine. Heck, I never even spoke to her.

Breasal is enraptured at the sight. Now is the time to escape. I'm certain he's forgotten to lock the door to the main entrance. Now how in the name of all that's holy can I get out of this blasted cage?

After carefully examining every inch of this trap, I noted several breaks in the mesh that had been repaired with leather strips. I bet I can chew through them. Never tried before, but then I never had fox teeth before. I can do this. I drew back my lip and sunk my teeth deeply into the leather. It was thick but narrow. Shaking my head, I felt my teeth nearly meet. One more bite and I am through this piece. The next strip was one facing outside.

I was about halfway through the second piece when I looked skyward and saw Fiona flying soundlessly overhead. She made a shrill call, that we developed as a signal not too long ago. I understood her message and continued to gnaw. Suddenly, I was free. The last piece of leather still in my teeth, I scampered out of the building and ran towards the castle.

I don't remember Camelot being this far from Avalon, yet it seemed to take a vast amount of time. Fiona and I had a secret way of speaking when she was flying as she was too far away when she flew. Barely able to put one paw in front of the other, I was a short way from the cemetery, I hoped Fionna would remember where she had last seen me. I blacked out and collapsed to the ground.

~ ~ ~

Fiona

There is no time to waste. I'd seen where the kidnapper had hidden Elaine. I still cannot fathom why that fool little man took my Finn. Elaine, I understood. As High Priestess of Avalon would be more worth far more than a woodland creature.

I dare say no one has been in that mausoleum in many decades. How did this annoying man find it? It must have been an accident. It is hard to find something when you don't know what to look for.

I flew as fast as I could to tell Merlin and Morganna what I had seen.

Entering the castle, I heard the wizard and the priestess discussing what would be their next move.

I was barely through the door and noticed Arthur close behind me.

"Well, have you two found any answers? We must do something other than talk endlessly. We need a plan and act on it immediately."

"Please Arthur calm yourself," the wizard said, grasping the King's arm. Arthur shook him off angrily.

"Listen," I said, "stop bickering. I have information which should ease your concerns. Finn has been captured by that faux sorcerer and just now freed himself. We must go to the mausoleum."

Arthur interjected, "What mausoleum? There hasn't been a crypt anywhere in the land in many ages. What are you talking about?"

"I've seen it, right behind the graveyard at Glastonbury. It is a huge building. The door was open, and I saw Finn on top of a stone effigy, in a metal cage. He was chewing on some leather when I saw him. I am certain he is now free. I signaled to him that I would find him, once, I told you where he'd been."

The sorcerer turned, fire in his eyes. "Damn it, when I eradicated the mausoleums as far from the boggy lands around Glastonbury, none should remain."

"What should I do?" the king asked. "Do you want me to send Sir Bors out to tell them, the mausoleum will be taken down without regard to the persons within, if they do not comply at once and move the bodies to graves?"

"No!" Morganna cried.

"I was there just yesterday and there was no such structure behind the graveyard. It must be the doing of a wizard. If it is as large as Fiona says, it could not be erected in a single day, by mortal men."

Merlin sighed. "She is right, no man could construct such a large building within a single day. As far as I know, I am the only wizard in the area."

Suddenly, I heard water-soaked feet slapping against the stone floors of Camelot. I flew from the room out to the corridor and saw Chuck waddling toward me.

"Chuck, what are you doing here? I never saw you in the castle before." His features indicated this was no mere visit. Something dire was on the ground hog's mind. He continued and entered the war room.

"Wall, I ain't here fer pleasure," he drawled.

"Sumpin has happened. The marsh is a turnin blue. And not jest a little blue, it's blue as an angry sea. My guess is, that thar stranger, is the culprit."

Morganna dropped to her knees in front of the woodchuck and grabbed him by the shoulders. "Have you actually seen this stranger, Chuck? What does he look like?"

"He's kinder tall, like Merlin. Dresses fancy and he disappears, inter thin air. Soon as I gets near a good look, poof, he's gone."

Morganna looked perplexed for a moment, then horrorstruck. "Merlin, it has to be the fool who follows Elaine. I don't know what he wants with her, but she's frightened of him."

"Could it be him who has taken Elaine?" I asked.

"Could the kidnapping and the illness be the same crime?" Flying to Morganna's shoulder, I stared at Chuck, whose mouth had dropped open.

I was stunned. It was as if Chuck and I had the same revelation. I'd known the ground hog for many centuries, and in many forms. We had shared some experiences, we both remembered a time, very long ago, we had met this culprit before. Chuck cleared his throat, sat back on his haunches, and finally spoke.

"Merlin, does ya member thet feller long ways back, always thought he were as great a sorcerer as you? Always bragging on hisself. One time you named him Breasal the weasel, do ya member, huh?"

Merlin was standing at the window and pulling at his beard as he often did when pondering a problem. He turned and faced Chuck.

"I do, Chuck, though I cannot remember where or when."

"Wall, Fiona and I does. And I bet ya she evens members the blue concoction. Tell him gell. He needs ter know, sos we can fix this here mess."

~ ~ ~

Finn

It must have been a long time since I was unconscious, as I now saw sunset. I tried to get up but, was too dizzy. Sinking back to the ground, my stomach clenched, causing me to vomit. I'd not taken any water since Arthur said the water is what made the illness. Why? Why, was I now sick? I tried again to stand to no avail. I just pray Fiona will find me quickly.

Once again, I fell into darkness. When I woke Fiona stood before me. Morganna took me into her arms, and Merlin stood above. I know the wizard would be certain I caused this.

"Master Wizard, I assure you none of this was my doing. I escaped from Breasal's metal prison. And, I'd only gone a short way from the mausoleum when I fell sick. Fiona, tell them."

Merlin sighed and said, "I believe you, Finn. There is no question that you are a victim." He then bent over and picked up the piece of leather I'd been chewing on.

"Is this the strip you chewed on from the cage?"

"Yes, it is, but it was not colored blue when I bit it. I thought it might help if I brought it to Merlin."

Morganna set me down carefully and took the strip from the Merlin. "Merlin, this is the same shade of blue as we saw so long ago."

Chuck waddled up and says, "Yer right, my lady, it's the same. I saw it when you two did and I also seed it ways before ya."

Merlin took it back from her and examined it more closely. "You are correct, my dear, it is the same. Finn, are you feeling better? We must handle this quickly, but you must rest for a while, we need you at your best if we are to correct all that has been done."

"Hey thar, you two ain't listenen, I told ya I seed it afore. Lotsa times and I seed how it were made and what it does," Chuck interjected.

I had listened carefully to all that was being said. "We need Harriet's mead, lots of it. Morganna, do you remember, to the letter, the incantation to destroy poison?"

She looked sky ward her features indicated she was trying to recall the words of the spell. Morganna gritted her teeth.

"No, no, no, I do not. And I threw away my spell book, once in a fit of anger. Oh, Fiona, what shall we do?"

Merlin paced, back and forth, over and over. "Well, Morganna, it seems that once again your temper has gotten us in an untenable situation. I will search my tomes and see if I can find the incantation. First, we must be certain Finn is well enough to save us. We will take him to my quarters. Fiona, you stay with me, and Morganna, fetch Harriet and bring as much mead as you can carry. Chuck, you will have to assist me."

Chapter 10

Chuck

"Iffen this don't beat all. Whatcher need, Merlin?"

"Well, old friend, what we need is your expertise. I lied when I told Morganna that I'd seen it done many times. She is right, it does take a unique skill. A skill that only you, among us all, can do re-animation of changelings. And, also how dangerous the task is. You have been here many centuries. You do understand what must take place?

"Yep, I does. And do yer amamaber, Master Wizard, yer gonna be changed for the remainder of your life?"

"I do, Chuck. And I deeply regret that I shall never again see you." The wizard sighed deeply and shed a single tear.

"Thank ye. I will miss ya as well, but always amember, you can call upon me at any time. And it will be wonderful to see some of my old friends, that have entered the same promised land."

The old man had tears in his eyes and the bird flew to his shoulder and leaned her head against him. It has been eons since I have been a man. A man who deeply loved a woman. A woman who is long dead.

"Let's get on with it, can't be awastin time now," I said as tears were forming in my eyes.

So many of my friends have passed to the place I now long for. Figgers, I been here for seven thousand years. I seen lots a things and helped lotta folks.

Arthur spoke up. "And what is it I am supposed to do?" Merlin spoke softly to the King.

"Leave."

"Leave? Listen, I am King here. This is my kingdom. Whatever happens I will know about it." Arthur was clearly angry, on the cusp of rage. He started pacing and slammed his right fist into his left hand. It startled us. Morganna had left and did not hear the slapping sound.

Merlin was standing by the open window, he turned, glared, saying, "You will leave now, Your Highness, or you shall have no kingdom."

Arthur, began to sputter, "But, but... I am regent. The words I speak are law."

Merlin spoke again, very softly. "You do not make natures law, nor do I. However, important you believe yourself to be, is but a mere drop in the bucket of nature. Leave, at once."

The King left, grumbling and shuffling his feet. He slammed the door yet said not a word.

As the door closed, Fiona said, "Master Merlin, what is it you would have me do?"

Merlin sighed deeply. "You each play a part. We are all of the magic."

I too was surprised. I knew Morganna was a priestess but was not aware she held sorcery as well.

Merlin combed his beard with his fingers and gently smiled. "Finn, you and Chuck will go back to the mausoleum. Elaine will still be sleeping, so make as little noise as possible. I shall be watching and will instruct you once you reach the building. Are you certain Finn, you are well enough to handle this?"

"If I am magic, I believe I can handle whatever you want me to do. Thank you for your faith in me."

Finn was now contrite, I knowed he was the right feller, right frum the getgo.

The wizard drew back his shoulders and stood taller than I had ever seed him. "Chuck, have you selected the proper theater for this?"

"I has. Now yer gots to understand, ya has ta do whatever I say. Each one is of prime importance. This ain't no game. It gots ter be done in a special way and I'm the only feller here thet can do it."

Merlin interjected, "Fiona, I am sure you comprehend what must be done. Finn, you are new to this, so listen carefully to Chuck, and do whatever he says? Just do what Fiona does. It is vastly important but, truly not dangerous, though it make look that way. Can you handle it lad?"

Finn was struck dumb. His mouth fell open as he nodded, his eyes were wide open.

"Well, boy, can yer do it?" I had to ask, cause iffen he missteps we could be in a heap a trouble.

The fox found his tongue. "Yes, Master Chuck, I can."

I smiled. *I kinda knew he'd be all right. I does like it when anyone calls me Master Chuck. Been here a buncha time, but have to say this is the best time. Gonna miss these folks.*

"Okay, then follar me. We gots a way ter go and it's getting near dusk. It's too darn dark already. Well, let's prepare as much as we can tonight and go in the morning."

~ ~ ~

Fiona

I was certain Merlin would get to the bottom of this. It seems somewhat strange that Chuck has apparently more knowledge than the Master Wizard. Maybe he has been here far longer than I believed. If Merlin says to do as Chuck says, I will follow his directions.

"Master Chuck, what would you have me do?" I asked.

"Little gell, yer gots the most important part. So, what yer gots ter do is fly overhead and tells me ther moment ya sees the things I tells ya to find. Don't worry about how ter signal me. Ya'll hear me voice in yer head. And I'll hear yours."

Merlin appeared puzzled. He started to walk, back and forth, in front of the marsh. He wrung his hands and pulled at his beard. When he was angry, he sometimes paced, or wrung his hands, but not in all the years I've known him, never did I see him do all three.

"Hey thar, Missy, pay attention. I told ya twice now, what ter do."

"I'm sorry, Chuck. I noticed that Merlin seems conflicted. Should he be paying attention as well?"

"Wall. Fer the moment, we ill jest let him do what he wants."

The ground hog seemed to reach into his pocket, that I was certain he did not have, and extracted what appeared to be a large map. He set it on the ground and smoothed it out with his paws. I looked at it carefully and noted there were several locations marked with stars. I leaned over and placed my beak on one star.

"Dad bern it gell, you is one smart falcon. Thet is the last place yer have to see. Does ya recognize it?"

"I do, though I've not been there in some time. It very hard to fly in those canyons. Is that where I am supposed to go first?"

"Nah, thets is whar we must end up. Now foller my paw and you will see the way we gots ter go." Chuck spoke with an authority I'd not heard before.

I looked down and felt Finn beside me. Chuck often directed me to a certain spot, but I'd never before been part of a team. "Finn, are you coming with me?"

The fox smiled and nodded yes. I will find the task much easier with him by my side.

"Chuck," I inquired, "Am I to fly far above or close to the ground, so that Finn can help me?"

"Both," he responded. "Yer gonna be up and down. I'll tells ya when ter change."

"Change? You mean change my form?"

"No, no gell jest change yer course. Now thisin is a dangerous and long trip. Are ya both ready for it? Thar is a lots ridin on the four of us. We gots ter move quickly, gots to be thar exactly at midnight."

Finn spoke up. "Chuck, it is dark now. If it is long and dangerous we will never make it on time."

"Thets right, Finn, but I wants ter make certain, ya'll understand this here trip. Ain't easy ya know. So we all will stay in Merlin's quarters and leave at fust light. We gots ter travel dang near five days."

I flew up to a high cabinet where Merlin had placed furs. Chuck watched me as I quickly made myself comfortable. He and Finn found a pallet, and both were fast asleep within moments.

This was not going to be as simple a task as I thought. We didn't bring any provisions. How will we eat and what are we to sleep on? I didn't dare question Merlin. as he was cross. The old man does not like to travel, let alone for five days.

I pondered the problem for several moments, then decided to let the masters handle this alone. My task is just to do as Chuck and Merlin say. Then I drifted off to sleep, knowing they will handle any situation that appears.

I heard Finn yawn. It was morning already? I barely remember going to sleep, I flew down beside him. He sat back on his haunches and kicked his head, in the same manner as a cat.

I laughed at him. He turned toward me and shook his head. "Are you prepared for whatever must come? I don't think this is going to be easy."

"I know we don't have any provisions. If this is going to take five days, we have to eat, don't we? You and I can hunt, but Chuck will be too busy and at this point I think Merlin is disgusted with the whole thing."

"Yeah, I've never seen him this grumpy."

Just then a small cart pulled by a donkey appeared. Merlin clapped his hands together and a table was on the ground, heavily laden with food. I guess the wizard has gotten over his grouchiness.

Chuck waddled toward the food and set himself down on a bucket that was overturned. Seats were provided for each of us, in the manner we required. Merlin sat at the head of the table in a large chair. He cleared his throat and bowed his head, and said, "Pray for us Priestesses of Avalon and Druids throughout the land that we might complete this mission as we are directed. And bless this food placed before us."

He said nothing more throughout the meal, other than to place the table and chairs onto the donkey cart. Which we did after we had eaten.

Dadburn it, the old Wizard has gots kinda moody over the years. I don't think I should tolds him all of this journey. Tain't easy, this living fer nigh on to forever. I think he's worried about thet other wizard taking his place.

Merlin came to me where I was asitten on a fallen log near the fire. Finn and Fiona was atalkin on the tuther side of the flames. He sets down aside me, adjusts his robe, clears his throat, and starts talking ter me.

"Chuck, I fear I am not up to the task. I am afraid. For the first time. I am not sure of what action I should take. Please tell me what is in store for me?

"Merlin, we's knows each other fer a long, long time. Yer, gonna be fine. This ain't my fust time at this show, ya know. Listen, I unnerstan, yous nervous, but amamber I'm gonna takes good care of ya. Now goes to sleep, we gots a tough day aheada us."

The old man pushed his hands into the armholes of his robe and walked to his tent. What Finn and Fiona found in the wagon and put up fer us, a tent and provisions for the day. Theys good kids, they ain't got a scare in any of thar bones. I'd like ter tell um what theys afacin but the council ain't gonna like thet. Best not.

I waved ter the "kids" and told em to get much shut eye as they ken. I twern't worried cause even I knew, they could handle it, even as this would be the toughest ter get thru, worsen theyd ever seen afore.

I heard Fiona a messin around trying ter find some grub. Sos I gets up to help her. Shes aleanin over ther side of the donkey cart a tryin ter find sumthin ter eat. Wall she comes up with a bag and a small bale of hay.

"Hi, gell. I'll feed Amadeaus. You fix us all sumpin."

I takes the hay from her and pulls off an amount what the donkey needs. She opens the bag and shakes her head yes. Good gell, that one. Finn woke as he heared me and Fiona fixin grub fer usen.

"Them banocks ain't gonna stay hots fer very long boy, gets a move on."

Finn grabbed the blanket in his teeth and pulled it off hisself. He gots up and seys thet is what he was afixin ter do, afore I said so.

"Dad-burned youngens know it all," I muttered.

~ ~ ~

Merlin

I have never before felt this way. Maybe it is old age, after all I am seven thousand years on this planet. I wish I knew what Chuck has in store for me. All of us have something we wish never happened. My regret box is overflowing.

I noticed everyone else was awake. Even the dang donkey seems to have a full belly. I walked over to the table and saw a place for me had been set.

"Good morning, everyone. Seems a fine day to begin our journey."

Fiona said, "We hope the rest of the day goes well." Finn nodded, his mouth full of bannocks. Chuck seemed to be pouring over the map I'd seen yesterday.

"Well, Master Chuck, where do we start?" He pointed to a star on the map, took a piece of coal from the now extinguished fire, he drew a line from the star he pointed to and then another location. I really did not want to go to the first star.

I recall the battles that were fought there, many times. It is not a pleasant place. I dare say it yet bares the stench of the last conflict.

Chuck apparently noted my discomfiture, as he said, "Well, Merlin, this first step is the hardest and it is yer duty to face it alone."

"Alone? Why? I thought this mission effects all of us."

"It does. Ya'll hasta deal with yer own personal demons. Since you are the oldest, you will go fust.

Master Merlin, you dunt look like yer really don't wanna go on this mission. Whtcha afeared of? Fer cripes sake, yer the most powerful wizard in the land. Yer know you gonna bees all right."

Chuck could see my insecurities. "I assure you my fear is not for my person but, my mind. I fear the memories will drive me insane."

"Wall, Merlin, old friend, thet is purty silly. Your mind has brung ya this far, it ain't gonnen any whars. Now buck up, man. Yer don't wanna scare the youngens, do ya?"

"I'm not sure my fear will touch them," the old man replied. "They are young, they stare trepidation in the eye and carry on."

"Yer might be right about Finn, but Fiona has been here near as long as you. She's twitterpated bout him. I don't think she ever thinks bout anythin but him."

"You are correct, Chuck. I'm being foolish n selfish. Give me a few moments, then I will be ready to proceed. Thank you, I owe you much."

~ ~ ~

Finn

Poor old man, I have never seen him look so,.. not really frightened, but he sure is concerned. Maybe this mission isn't the adventure I thought it to be. However, neither Fiona or Chuck seems to be feeling as cautious as the wizard.

Fiona was perched on the edge of the cart and the dang donkey was stomping his feet and shaken his tack, Chuck waddled toward us, "Youens ready? Come on, Finn, get into the cart. We gots a lot a trail ter cover."

I thought I would be racing alongside the small conveyance.

"You want me in the cart too?"

"Yep, we'll be travelin fer quite a spell afore we reach the fust obstickle. Bout five hours. And I need yer to be in fighten shape, jest in case I need ya."

Would we possibly run into bandits? Is someone following us? Maybe that other wizard is dangerous.

Merlin approached, his robe looked as if it had been recently cleaned, his beard almost glowed, it was so white. You might think he was going to a grand ball, instead of a mission to save the kingdom. I jumped up into the conveyance. Fiona walked on the edge and settled beside me. The old man jumped in with the vigor of a young man. He leaned over the edge and assisted Chuck as he tried to get aboard.

~ ~ ~

We had been riding for hours. Chuck and Fiona were apparently rocked to sleep with the action of the swaying cart. It was nearly noon even the poor donkey was sleepy. The animal stopped, and Merlin looked to me as he exited the rickety wagon. "I'll feed the tired donkey, and you can rustle up something for us to eat," he said, as he grabbed some hay from the head of the cart. I found some cheese, bread, and apples in the sack.

I laid out the food as best as possible. "Well, Finn, you have done a fine job."

"Thank you, sir. I'm trying. All of this is a bit strange for me. But I'll do whatever you and Chuck think is best. I think I hear the others stirring. Would you please get them, so I can keep the bugs way?"

"Of course, but I see them coming, so no need."

As Fiona sat beside me, I feel the heat of her body. *Though we are different animals, perhaps by some miracle we can be together.*

Chuck approached his large feet making slapping noises as he walked, his rump moving from side to side. "Hi, thar, ya'all ready fer today? Now don't worry none. It's tough, but yer can all handle it."

Merlin left the table without having et. He was a getting thet worry face again. Best tell him sumpin ter raise his sprits. Cain't have em chickening out on the fust go around.

I moved from the table grabbing an apple as I left. Puttin my paw on his side, I sezs, "Listen here, 'MR.' Wizard, you gots to do this. We aren't a gonna give up this here mission, cause of yer feelins. You sets here, and get yer mind aworken, like its surpose ter. Now eat sumpin, else yer goona wish yer did."

I was surprised. I thought Merlin was our leader, yet it is Chuck that was giving orders. I mean, dang it, he's an old man. Why can't I go first? I'm young, and not afraid.

I took some cheese and walked over to the ground hog, as he sat at the table. "Chuck, I can see Merlin is concerned about this first trial. Why can't I go first? If he sees that it will be done without harm, he'll step up and go through the next."

The sorcerer knelt beside me and put his hand on my shoulder. "I thank thee for the offer, Finn, but I have been commanded to do this, otherwise the whole of Camelot and all our king has made will disappear."

Wow, this is much more serious than I first believed. I think it will be best for me to keep my mouth shut. Fiona flew from the seat at the table and landed beside me. She closed her eyes and nodded. She agreed.

"Wall, folks, eat yer fill we needs ter get startin, cain't waste time. This fust test is the toughest, and if you have full bellies, it will be easier. Okay?"

I went back to the table and took more cheese and an apple. Going over to the bundle of food I found some feed for Fiona. Takin up as much as my paw would hold. *She is small, but feisty and she'll need sustenance to go further.* I waddled up to the wagon.

~ ~ ~

Morganna

"Harriett, you don't know how much this helps your king and country. I am so sorry we need so much, but you will be amply compensated."

"I understand, my lady, anything to save us all from this plague."

The dear lady did not know that it was not in fact, an illness. I think it is best not to tell her. She also provided a wagon to transport the casks. I wish more folks were like Harriett. She is kind and selfless.

"Harriett, you are far more lady than I. Trust me you and yours will not go hungry."

We arrived at the castle and were directed to the postern gate as the casks were too wide to go through the front entrance. The poor mare was struggling with the additional weight. "Only a few more feet, you sweet girl. And you will be fed the finest Camelot has to offer."

The mare looked back at me as if to say, "There better be." As we reached the gate, we heard it creak open and several young lads began to unload the mead. One took the mare's reins and to lead her to the stable. I yelled to him, "Give her the best of food and care. Treat her as if she is Arthur's steed."

The boy nodded and led her away. Harriet started to unload the casks. "No, dear lady, they are too heavy for a woman. The lads will unload and inform Arthur it is here. You have toiled enough, please, go home and have a cup of tea." She looked at me in astonishment. Poor woman has worked herself from before sunrise, to long after sunset.

"Thank you, my lady. I dare say I could use the rest. Perhaps I will sit in the sun and nap."

"You certainly deserve it. I will have Arthur send supper for you and your daughter."

I never have felt such contentment, simply from helping someone. No wonder the peasants are always aiding one another. Arthur is responsible for this. The man knows how to care for his subjects. I headed back to the castle to inform him we had completed our task and Chuck was under way.

He was not in his quarters, so I searched and found him in the war room. He was conferring with Sir Bors. The knight was one of the best tacticians in Arthur's army. I knocked at the casement of the open door. "Pardon me, gentlemen, may I enter?"

Arthur waved me over to the round table, where he had spread a large very well-drafted map. Sir Bors nodded his greeting to me.

"What are you searching for Your Highness?"

"We need to find out exactly the mausoleum is and if it is of magic or simply something that has been neglected and overgrown."

Sir Bors looked at me, a frown on his features. The man was pragmatic and not given to believing in magic.

"My king, what do you mean magic? Surely you cannot believe in such things."

"Bors, there are many things in this world, that we neither understand nor place faith in, but nevertheless we must not dismiss, simply because we don't understand," Arthur replied.

"If you say so Sire," Bors replied and turned back to face the map. He then turned and faced the king.

"Arthur," he said, "Look, there is enough space to place a large building behind the cemetery. I think this the place you mean."

I had to speak up. "Arthur, Sir Bors, I was there the day before it was discovered. At that time there was nothing there. Not a single structure, not even a garden shed. Has anyone spoken to the priests? If the building could appear in a single day, or less, surely they would hear something."

"Yes, sister, they should have heard something if it were not of magic. However, in view of all we have learned, we must assume it is enchanted. There can be no other explanation."

Though I did not want to believe it, I knew his deduction was accurate. I wonder if Elaine is complaisant. She can be devious, but I doubt she would give up her lofty position to aid one who would destroy Camelot. I must find her and quickly.

~ ~ ~

Elaine

I must get out of here. This man is not a lover, of me or anyone. I am not overly fond of my husband, but he is a good man and I would never cuckhold him. Nothing this man provides in the way of food or drink, do I dare touch. I think he is trying to poison me. But why? I have nothing of value that does not belong to Avalon. Everyone knows priestess's own nothing, save what is gifted to them. Trinkets and flowers. What thief would want such things?

Hearing his footsteps, I eased back down on the pillows. He entered with a pitcher of what appeared to be water. However, it seems to be too vivid a blue to just be water. He poured some of the liquid into a glass and offered it to me.

"No, thank you, I'm fine now." I sat up and extended my arms wide and swept the chalice from his hand, it landed and crashed into a thousand shards of glass. Then pushing aside, the bedcoverings I pretended to get out of the bed. "Oh, I'm so sorry. I've broken your beautiful cup. Please let me clean it up."

The look of pure rage that flashed over his features made him look like a monster. He took a deep breath and quickly composed himself.

"No, my dear," he said between clenched teeth, "I handle it, you must rest."

"No, no, I'm quite rested, I shall clean it up. After all, it is woman's work." I dare not let him see the rage he'd instilled in me. He'd tipped his hand, I'll not let him tip mine.

"I'll be back in a moment dear. I need to get something to clean this... mess... accident up. Wait for me here. I shan't be long."

"And who is it I shall be waiting for? You may have mentioned your name but for heaven's sake I have forgotten. I'm sorry, silly me."

He seemed to now have a better demeanor. Let him think I'm an idiot, I'm not as stupid as people think I am. It is a protection for me, to appear witless and I get others to do what I don't want to. He will be back soon, I have to take this opportunity, else I will perish here.

I gathered what little I had with me and headed for the sunlight. I was no more than free of the building than I saw him approaching. Fortunately, he did not see me. Taking off my boots that could be noisy, I hitched up my skirt and ran from the old oak tree that hid me from his sight. I must get to Morganna before he finds me. She will know what I must do to rid myself of this dangerous man and save the kingdom from the weird blue poison. I must step up and do the right thing.

The postern gate was wide open. Probably for the merchants that come on this day. There is no way I can blend in with them, so I eased myself down into the marsh and applied mud to my gown. Thankfully, the mud dried quickly, and I was able to brush away the globs of dirt and thus I looked like any other woman from the village.

Once in the castle I headed toward Morganna's quarters. She was not there, but I heard her voice, coming from the next room. I knocked on that door and all speech stopped. The King bid me enter.

"Morganna!" I cried and ran to embrace her.

"You have to help me. Someone kidnapped me, and I am sure he added the poison to the well on Avalon."

"You were kidnapped! How did you get away?" Morganna asked.

Arthur turned from the war table saying, "Elaine, who took you? Are you injured? How can we help you?"

Morganna continued to hold me in her arms. She motioned the regent over to her, saying, "We must find Merlin. This situation is more than I can bear alone. I shall stay with her and you must find the wizard."

For some reason, the King became angry. "No, you have more powers than I for searching out the mage. I'll remain here with Elaine."

"Why, Arthur? You have more resources than I. There are no knights to do my bidding."

"True, but Merlin is not angry with you. I've been told to remain here until he returns. Imagine. He gave ME orders. I am the king, am I not?"

I sense our fine king is jealous. That explains his anger. But this is not a matter of vanity, but one that can quite quickly annihilate us all.

"I am most certain, he wished you to stay within the castle for a reason," I replied.

"Personal feelings do not generally effect the sorcerer's directions."

Arthur lowered his head to his chest. "You are quite correct, Elaine. Sometimes I am a foolish regent. However, I will do as he's told me, and you will find him. I will wait here with Elaine. Is that all right with you, Priestess?"

I smiled. I did not wish to upset the king. "Yes, Your Highness, your company would be most welcome, as the last man I stayed with was both mean and cruel. Which, Sire, you are not."

"Thank you, Elaine," he said, smiling, "I know you are humoring me, but it is much appreciated."

Morganna released me, grabbed a shawl, threw it across her shoulders, and left.

~ ~ ~

Chuck

It will be difficult for all of them. This long dark tunnel is not to my liking either. I shook Fiona, placing my paw over my mouth to indicate she was not to wake the others.

"Listen, gell. We's almost thar. I wants yer to fly overhead and sees what we's afacin. Kin yer do that kinder quick like and don't make ter much noise? Come back and tells me what yer sawed. But don't say it loud like, Merlin must face thisin on his ownself."

Thet beautiful falcon took flight and through the tunnel she went. *I hope the end of this here trial will make things much better for all of us.*

It seemed only moments that she returned. "Chuck, that is the most disgusting thing I've ever seen. How will Merlin be able to handle this?"

"He has ta, gell. Needs ter rid em of these fears whats aholding him back. He is a powerful mage, but he is also a man. A great man to be sure, but nevertheless still a mortal man."

He musta heared our voices, cause the Merlin was awake. He came over to our group from the warmth of the fire.

He smiled, saying, "Is this a private party or may anyone join?"

I was a little upset with him. I knew he was trying to make light of a situation. "'Tis far from a party, Merlin. This is probably the most demanding task of your complete attention. It is not to be taken likely." *I must remember to appear as a poorly speaking ground hog. I can't reveal myself too soon.*

The wizard bowed to me and then shook his head. "I realize how difficult this matter to be, but I was trying to lift my spirits. This is a field I hoped never to see again. It is the most frightening thing I have ever seen in my many years."

"I too know, this trial is the worstest I eva seed."

"You mean you have already seen what I must encounter, and you have not told me?"

"Me telling ya, would violate the contract tween me and the elders. Listen here, boy, you are not the only mage in the country. Yer hafta face thisen alone. Can't tell yer what's ahead nor aid ya in any fashion."

He did not reply. He simply walked to the cart and took some food for Amadeaus. Yet not even an apple or cheese for himself.

Finn stood in the cart and shook himself. It was part of his routine. Ever morning jest like this. Shakes, eats, and asks what he is to do for the day. This day was no exception.

"Morning, Chuck. Is the wizard able to face his mission? He didn't seem happy about it last night. I can do it, let the old man sit this one out."

"Finn, I know you can, but he MUST!" *I wern't gonna have da same conversation with anyone else. I heard meself say it too dang many times.* "Now get, yer time ill come."

Merlin finished feeding the donkey and asked, "Must I walk to the field or are we all going in the cart?"

"You'll walk. The rest of us will wait, until you are halfway in der field." "You will not drown me, will you?" he asked, trepidation in his tone.

"No, thet would be purty stupid, wouldn't it?" Sometimes even sorcerers are dumb as a pile of dung. "Neva mind, the task on yer mind. Jest step up and do yer duty." Merlin returned to his tent, sulking.

"But Finn said he could do it. Why not let him?" *I had no ideer the old feller would be this ascaret. I cain't let the old man, jest rest. He's gots ter to it hisself.*

"Merlin, gets yerself out here and face me."

The mage stuck his head out from the tent and said, "I can't go on."

I cursed and grew quickly to the height of seven feet. I could feel my eyes enlarging and growing red. My paws I clenched into fists.

"Now go, or I shall plant you in this horrid ground forever!"

Fear-stricken, Merlin stepped onto the field. He tried to walk, but the mud eased itself up onto the wizard's leg, and he became immobile.

"Stop doubting yer ownself. You can and will do it." Once again, I shall show him my ire. I clenched my paws and rose above him.

He pulled his foot from the mire, then the other. His confidence grows with each step. He is crying and smiling, and he starts to run. It appears the mire is deeper in the center, but the wizard pushes on. He's overcome his fears. I watched him across the field of mud, blood, human beings decapitated, and limbs strewn everywhere. Though he is deeply saddened to view so many that he had advised Arthur, to send to war are now floating in muddy blood and limbo, he realizes, so many died for so little, and he was able to carry on, as was his duty.

I directed Finn and Fiona into the cart, and we circumvented the field and met the old man on the other side. He was still shaking, but not because of fear, but the darkness brought with it chilling winds. We were all tired and cold and anxious to get back to our camp. The return trip was over far more quickly than the outgoing one. "Go into your tent, Merlin. Change your sodden clothing and warm yourself."

The others did as I directed and hurried to get warmer clothing as well as the Mage. "I'll feed Amadeaus and meet you at the table."

He no more than turned, than the table appeared fully prepared with delicious food. I knew it was Merlin who provided the elegant repass. His trial had gained him much, as to facing his fears and learning you must do your part so the team shall win.

All left to their respective tents, save Finn.

He looked at me, his mouth agape. "Master Chuck, what has happened?"

I forced myself to return to my natural size and laughed. "Fear not, lad, for fear is our greatest enemy. Merlin has overcome his. And now, my young friend, it is your time to defeat yours."

"Mine? But, I fear nothing."

"I think not, Finn. You always stayed around the marsh, but never went in the water. Why is that? Fear, I figgers."

"But how did you know? I never said I wanted to swim, not even when I was bored, when I first came to Camelot."

Chapter 11

Morganna

I knew I had to find her. Who knows what that idiot Breasal will do to her? He can't believe Avalon would pay a ransom for her. She is probably scared out of her wits. Bad enough he might hurt her, but as frightened as I believe her to be, she may harm herself.

For a certainty she is not at Camelot. I will search all the area around the castle and then to Avalon and the monastery. I ran from the castle and was hit by an epiphany. Before this crisis, things had been quite calm at the castle and at Avalon, and I used my powers far less than I ought. Completely forgotten was the fact that I did not have to physically search if she was in England. I hope I can remember the incantation. Now to find water. The marsh is too murky, and I would do well to return to the calm water of Avalon. Yet, if the water is poisoned, it may not work.

By all that is holy, what am I do to? Scrying is the easiest and fastest way, but I fear water that is tainted will not work. I fell to the ground kneeling, placed my hands over my eyes and began to sob. All at once I felt something on my knees. As I opened my eyes, my tears caused my vision to shimmer. I wiped at my face with the hem of my robe. Yet the tears continued to flow. I touched my face then felt the moisture. It was not salty. There balanced precariously on my knees was a shallow alabaster bowl. So white it seemed to glow. From my eyes the water sought the bowl, the stream did not make the ripples that usually appear when liquid is poured into a shallow vessel. When the bowl was filled, a mist formed then, within, I saw Elaine. She is hiding in the monastery. It looks to be a small room with curtains that were closed.

I quickly left the castle grounds and headed for the lake that surrounded the abbey and Avalon. As frightened as she is cowering in the small room, she retained a grace that I'd not seen in her before. She almost seems as if she has become a woman, and not the foolish lass I knew.

I ran as fast as I could to the edge of the lake. The ferryman was waiting for me, though I had not whistled for him. Jumping into the flat-bottomed boat, I stood at the prow. Raising my arms overhead, I placed my palms together. Then I turned them and slowly lowered my arms to my sides.

The small dark man poled the boat to the shore just below the Canterbury church. Thanking the man, I climbed up the knoll, then entered the church. As I had never been inside before, I looked all around and found nothing that resembled what I saw in the alabaster bowl.

A monk in a soft grey robe came up to me, saying, "My dear, are you lost?"

"No, sir, not lost, simply confused. I believe my friend is within your church."

He smiled and gently took my arm and led me to a long bench. Together we sat.

"Do you know if your friend has been here before? I have seen a lady dressed in the same fashion as you about a week ago."

"Did you speak with her? Did she appear frightened?"

"No, my lady, she came for confession. She spoke to Father Paul." He pointed to a crimson curtain that seemed to cover a small room. *It was as I had seen in the scrying vessel.*

"Father Paul will have more to tell you about her. I shall fetch him for you." The monk left the area, and as soon as he was out of earshot, I heard a strange hissing sound.

Psst, psst came from the room behind the curtain. It was almost funny, except this is no laughing matter. The curtains moved slightly, and I saw Elaine peek her head from between the curtains.

I hurried to her side. She was crouched into a corner as if she trying to make herself smaller.

"Morganna, thank the fates you've come. He drugged me and put me in a fancy room. It was so beautiful it would take your breath away. He tried to make me drink the poison. I'd seen him put in the well. But before that he told me I needed water. That's when he brought me the

poison. Then I played like I was fine and threw my arms wide. And…
I broke the chalice and for an instant he got real angry. And then, then
he said he would clean it up and get me more. So, when he left, so did
I. I really did not know where to go, so I came here as it was closest. I
hoped someone would be here and he wouldn't risk coming in."

I nodded and held her close. "Elaine, there is trouble that Merlin
and Chuck are handling. We must find them at once."

"Where is Arthur? He usually is with them," she replied. The poor
woman was puzzled. Yet, she sounded more in control of herself.

"I was just with him. He said Chuck told him he must stay behind."
Again, confusion fell over her face.

"Chuck? Who's Chuck?"

"Elaine, I do not have the time to explain Chuck. You will find
out in due time. For now, we must return to Arthur. Come." She did
as I bid and stood beside me.

Father Paul entered and said, "Elaine, my dear, you appeared
fearful as you left. Have you been hurt?"

She shook the clergyman's hand, stood tall beside me as she told
him she was all right, and thanked him for his concern. Then we exited
the place I never thought I would enter.

"Morganna, I am truly sorry that I've led you to believe I am timid,
sincerely I am sorry. But the truth is I was never shy. I only pretend to
be to get my way. It always worked with my husband. However, he
was smarter than I gave him credit for. That is the reason I left him
and came to the Isle. It met no close attention on Avalon. Thus, I was
able to get things done for me, rather than having to do them myself."

"Elaine, that is rather childish. You know we always support our
priestess. How long did you expect this tactic would work?"

"Morganna, you know me all too well. I wanted the power you have.
But now I believe you should be the High Priestess. I am not qualified.
Not only because I deceived you. But your knowledge and memory are
outstanding. I will never be able to do anything as well as you."

"You are a foolish priestess, that is true, but even the elders were
not fooled by this deception. I was angry with you for a time, but it no
longer troubles me. The elders chose you for a reason quite unknown
to me. It is not my business to quiz them about something that is
none of my concern."

"I understand, Morganna, but let us find Merlin and assist him with the mystery of the blue-colored water, find out why he is on some mission."

~ ~ ~

Chuck

Wall, we gots through thet one better than I thought we might. The old feller did great. I jest hope it doesn't go to his head. Thet's all I need, an uppity wizard.

I slapped my paw against the table. "Listen, folks, we don't have ter travel far fer thisen, River's right ahind us."

Finn looked at me, fear flooding his features. "Master Chuck, if we needn't travel could we do it right away?"

I kinda figgered thet he'd be anxious to get over with it.

"Finn, I gets how ya feels, but you will need rest and food. Now, gets yer ownself ter the table and eat your fill. Then, gets yer tail ter your tent and sleep. Thet is an order!"

"But, Chuck, it is still light out. We could do it and have an extra day to arrive precisely at midnight."

"No, Finn, I'm running this here show. You'll do as I sez. Thet is ther end of it."

Apparently, the others overheard and were eating in silence. Once they wer dun, they packed up the dishes and the table, and went to the tents without ser much as a good night. Wall, good, nows I can gets some rest my ownself.

Little do they know the river behind us is shaller, but the current is strong. Tonight is the only time in seven hundred years, will the current flow with the greatest of power in ther opposite direction. This may or may not show Finn, he must use his own head and fergets bout what others done said. I hope he is not overly fearful. He's seed Merlin, endure his trial, and he cain't be a sissy in front of his ladyfriend.

The night passed quickly. I did not dream, that I can remember, and I feel invigorated. When the others woke we all heard the rapidly running river. Thet sound were loud and somewhat strange. The water ran hard and swift, gathering force as it moved against the stones, instead of flowing over them, as was the way for decades.

The entire camp was quieter than any dern mouse. Only noise I hear is Fiona's gentle like snore. Ther rest of um is sleeping quiet.

The night passed quick. Soon as my head hit ther piller I went right ter la- la land. Guess others did to. I gots up and found Fiona putting together a break-fist fer us. I spoke softly telling her I'd feed Amdeaus and be at ther table shortly.

The falcon nodded and continued her task.

Merlin awoke next, followed by a reluctant Finn. Merlin was trying to relieve the fears of the poor fox. Hard enough to cross a dangerous river as a lad, but near impossible for a frightened fox. 'Twer a good thing to try to help, but he's gots to face thisen on his ownself.

"Lets us get this here show on the road. Gots to clean up the camp dern't leave anything that will show we uns were here," I directed. I don't wants anyone ter see any remainder and follar us. The Ancients want this here mission to be known by nobody.

When everthin were packed up and into the wagon. We all walked ter the river, we could hear the rapidly running river. Sound were kinder loud, but strange. The water ran hard and swift, gathering force as it moved against the rocks. In the past the water flowed gently over the rocks thet time had eroded. Today it ran in a different manner. This strong and dangerous river would not be easy to cross.

Chapter 12

I wish I knew just why I am so afraid. I remember watching my friends swimming in the pond in the woods. They all seemed to be enjoying themselves, until... until.

My eyes grew wide and I became sick to my stomach. My stomach seemed to be crushed, until I could stand no more. I ran from the table to the edge of the river. It was moving so fast, and though I wanted to cry out for help the pain dropped me to my knees. I expelled every bit of food I had just eaten. There seemed to be more than I actually consumed. It was then and never before, that I finally realized the truth. The truth I'd told, no one, not even myself. It was Conor, my little brother. He was a skinny lad, as adventurous as the rest of the fellers. He'd try anything.

There were five of us, including Conor. We went into the woods to swim in the pond. Connor ran ahead, stripped, and was in the water before any of us. I had my shirt off and my shoes when I heard a scream from the water. I'd never seen a current in a pond before, but current or something like it was pulling Conor into swirling funnel-like thing.

I jumped in and reached for him. I could not touch him and in an instant my little brother was gone. The other boys fled to get help. But it was useless. Conor was gone, gone. The funnel disappeared and with it my brother.

I dressed quickly and went home. Never before had I hesitated to go home. I had a nice home, wonderful parents, but still I dreaded telling them what had happened. It was that same dread that filled me now. My mother never spoke after that day, becoming smaller and weaker each day. Until she too was gone. Gone to be with Conor.

Who can I tell? Who would not think I am a coward? I can't tell Fiona. And dealing with it on my own, hasn't helped me. Merlin could help, but his head was filled with his challenge overcome. That leaves only Chuck. He's kind of rough around the edges, but he has a big heart and might just understand.

The ground hog approached, waddling toward me with a towel in his paws.

"Yer feeling better? Sometimes thet cheese hits me the same way."

I took the cloth from him and dipped it in the water. After cleaning myself up, I watched to determine his mood. He sat on a nearby stump and appeared to be quite comfortable not at all anxious as he had been before when I left the table.

"Thanks for the towel, Chuck. I feel better now."

"Wall, yer gots sumpin ter tell me?"

I hesitated, drew in a great breath, and let the vile admission spew forth. Nothing did I hold back. The pain, the desolation, knowing I should have saved him. The tears were running down my face in a torrent.

Chuck picked up the towel, wrung it out and handed it to me.

I wiped my face and asked, "Do you understand how much this hurts? I've lived with it every day. Fiona has eased the feelings, but I can't tell her. Maybe if I can do this trial right, she might understand."

"Don't yer fret nun, Finn. I understand, yer don't think yer was serlected at random does ya? Them ancient fellers had yer pegged when yer was jest a little mite in yer cradle. Amember I told yer, I saw what the others didn't see? Them ancients gots good vision too."

"All right, Chuck, I shall follow your orders. But you must promise not to tell anyone what I've told you."

"Wall, Finn, thet would be a tough call, cause cept Fiona, everybody knows."

"King Arthur too?" I asked in a whisper.

"Wall, no he ain't one us."

"Not one of us. Do you mean he is against us?"

"Nah, he jest dern't have any special powers. Jest think about it Lad. Yer wasn't always a fox, Fiona is a bird and I t'wernt always a ground hog."

"Thet boy had a lot ter take in. His eyes were as big as saucers. His mouth fell open as if he had not control at all," I said aloud to myself, accounta no one else were around, cept Finn and he weren't listening.

Drat, I can't control this shaking on solid ground. What am I to do in the water?

"Chuck, can't you help me? You can change people. Can't you make water solid, you know, like ice in the winter?"

"Wished I could, Finn, but yer gots ter do what the ancients sez. I ain't loud to helps yer. Them thar is the rules. I cain't break em, yer cain't either."

"I'll do as you say, maybe something will come to me in a dream."

"Thet ther is quite possible, lad. Get yer sleep, and don't fret. You'll be jest fine. Now ter sleep."

I handed him the now-sodden towel and walked quickly to my tent, shaking my body to warm it and to rid myself of both fear and danger. *That was no easy route Merlin had to take. If he can do it, just maybe I can too.*

I thought I would never be able to sleep, yet the moment I lay on the blanket that served as my bed, I fell asleep.

Somehow, during my sleep I dreamt. Not of the water I feared, but of ground, dirt.

Was this the foretelling of my test? For I felt it was an answer. I went through the bushes to see what dangers I faced. Walking along the river's edge I came upon a huge limb that had fallen across the river. Unfortunately, the thin branches that I had hoped would reach the shore did not make it the entire way.

Suddenly my tent flew back and there before me was Chuck. "Yer all set, Finn? Amember you can do it."

Wow, that night passed quickly. After the dream I must have slept deeply.

"Yes, Sir, I am ready. I had a dream that I think will help me. Let me tell you."

"Nope, ain't gots the time. You have to start as soon as possible. No time fer dreams."

The river was creating a deafening noise. Yet for some reason, it was calling to me. *I can do this.* I was at the river's edge in advance of the others awakening. If I am lucky, perhaps I can do this before anyone really knows the task is complete. As the dream replayed in my mind, I walked down the path at the edge of the river. It seemed I walked forever before I saw anything that went over to the other side. Then just ahead, I saw the as the same I saw in my dream, a large log coming across to this side of the water. As in the dream the thin branches were mere twigs that would not hold my weight. *How can I bridge this? Bridge! That's it! I will build a bridge.*

There, directly in front of the branch, was a mound of dirt. I went to the pile and discovered it was not merely dirt but clay. I stood on the top of the pile with my back toward the edge of the shore and threw the clay with my forepaws, through my back legs. Soon I had a fairly tall mound of clay. I walked over to the clay and stomped on it until it was a firm solid mass. Then I went back to the clay pile and again and threw more of the substance upon the solid mass I had formed. It was taking time, but even if I finish after they wake, it will be a surprise. I dug deep into the clay tossing it upon the firm mound I had formed. It was now tall, but I needed it to bend over the twigs.

How? If I climbed upon it to the end I was sure it will topple. I looked all around the area, until I found another branch, this one was perfect. It was bent and appeared sturdy, it would do as a base for the clay. I pushed and pushed until I thought I was going to drop before I got the branch into the proper position.

Nearly exhausted, I leaned against the wood and it snapped into the very place I needed it to be. Now to apply the clay so it stays in place. Again, I went to the mound and threw the brown soggy mess as hard as I could to reach the place where the branches met. I had worked long and hard and was hungry.

Though the sun had not reached its highest point, much time had passed and no one from the campsite had sought me out. Why? I wondered.

I waited for some while for the clay to harden enough for me to walk on it. The base was sound, so I tentatively placed a paw on the newest portion of my bridge. It too was strong and held the branches firmly. If no one is here how can I prove I crossed the river? Should I go back, find them, or should I expect them to believe me if I am not wet?

My stomach began to growl, I was so hungry. After climbing to the point where the branches met, I noted a low-growing apple tree on the other side. I went over my bridge and grabbed an apple. Sitting down on my haunches, I munched on the tasty apple.

Also thirsty, I went to the edge of the river and leaned over the water. I fell into the churning waves and was ripped from the shore and thrown into the water that buffeted me from one rock to another. How will I live through this? Failure is not an option. Avery large branch was thrown against me as I weakly clung to a massive rock. The stone protruded above the water and I rose to the very top and reached out to the branch. It was too far from me, I strained and tried to reach it. Again, I was thrown onto the rocks. I grabbed another rock. It was smaller, but the top was quite flat. I laid on it and reached out to catch the tree limb. Holding it in my teeth as hard as I could, I pushed it to the opposite shore. Leaning at the point where the limb had been severed, I drove it into the far muddy river's edge.

Suddenly the cart appeared in front of me.

"How did you get here? I am sure my crude bridge would not hold for all of you and a cart."

"Wall, no, it dad burned wouldn't, but the large bridge bout two miles down did," Chuck replied.

"You mean if I had walked further, I could simply trot across an already- made bridge?"

"Yep, yer coulda. But, you needed to find a way to work around the problem and ya did so. Proud a ya, boy."

Merlin spoke up. "Finn, you have proved yourself worthy."

At once, the raging river calmed and flowed in the same manner it had seven hundred years before.

Chapter 13

Fiona

I hate it here. The wind is bitter and it changes whenever it feels like, making your task more difficult. This is not my first foray into this canyon. My first attempt was just an attempt. I failed miserably. The wind dashed me against the stone walls and beat me to a bloody pulp. It took me months to heal. I'm certain Merlin remembers as it was, he who nursed me. But I learned and determined if I am ever to endure this task again, I would emerge victorious. And today I shall do just that.

As I recall the wind near the top is less forceful, but the air is thin, and it is hard to breathe.

I may not be the finest bird in the rookery, but somehow I knew this test was coming. So, I practiced over and over. Frequently, when flying, I held my breath, so I could fly in thin air.

Chuck seems to think all I do is fly. Well, flying is not easy. Especially when nature is against you. But, I learned to make you way through the canyon, you ride the winds instead of letting them buffet you about. Today I will beat you, twisted canyon.

Suddenly a dark shadow cast over my path. I looked up and saw the largest bird I'd ever seen. I was clearly its prey. It dove over the rim of the canyon.

At once it was upon me, its talons digging deeply into my back. But this bird, no matter its size, had never before hunted here, as the wind dashed the massive falcon against the canyon wall. Dislodging its grasp on me.

The wind lifted me as I was free from the murderous clutches of the huge bird. The pain grew more intensive as I realized how badly I was injured. Will I be able to finish my trial?

Where before the winds had been against me, now they gently carried me to the ground.

Then everything went dark.

Chapter 14

Morganna

"Elaine, we must leave now!" She drew me down to her crouch and threw her arms about me in a vice like grasp. "Listen the bells are ringing for mass. Soon the church will be filled with parishioners. Come now, we must go." I stood and drew her up beside me. We walked out as if we were merely confessors.

Once free of the church, I led Elaine down the path toward the village of the little people. At least that was where I thought I was directing her. However, I was gravely mistaken. Nothing looked familiar.

It began to rain. Not a gentle pitter patter, this was a soaking rain that beat upon us. I felt drenched to the bone. The further we went, the harder it poured. Now we were not only lost, but wet and cold. I pulled my shawl over Elaine's shoulders. She nodded her thanks with a smile. This was new. I had never seen Elaine so calm and actually pleasant. This was a woman I do not know. Together, not speaking, we trudged onward.

The wind was now blowing fiercely, forcing our clothing to cling to our bodies. It seemed that everything was against us. I was ready to cry, yet Elaine retained her cheerful demeanor.

As cold as it had been, now it grew warm, and the wind seemed to raise toward a high bluff On the canyon we now found ourselves in, the heat grew intense, the sun poured its rays down upon us, and within moments we were dry.

Where are we? I had never before seen such a place. I don't know if I should be frightened or relieved.

Elaine smiled, folded the shawl, and handed it to me. "Well, this is much better, is it not?" she said.

I swear the woman grew several inches taller. There was a majesty I not seen on her before. She definitely was a High Priestess.

We walked into the canyon, not certain what we would encounter. But as Elaine is not fearful, why should I be?

We followed the curving wall of the stone chasm. It seemed to twist back upon itself. With every few steps, it again turned. It was as if we were following the trail of a snake. The priestess walked ahead of me and suddenly stopped.

"Morganna," she cried, "Look. Here is a fallen falcon. Could it be one of Arthur's? Can we help it?"

I recognized the bird at once. I examined her and found blood. So, she was injured. Her feathers we askew and she was breathing hard. I picked her up and gently to my breast. Within moments she stirred.

"What happened?" she asked, blinking her dark eyes at me.

"Fiona, it's me me, Morganna. Are you in any pain? You appear to be injured."

"It I just a simple wound that will keep me grounded for a bit. Nothing matters, save my failure. I don't know how I will face Merlin, Chuck, and Finn. They all endured hard trials. Mine was not that difficult, yet I cain't do it."

"Trials? What are you talking about? Why should they be disappointed in you?"

"I'm not sure I should tell you about the trials. This is all very foreign to me. I don't know what to do."

"Morganna! Put her down, she must finish by herself," was the cry high above us.

A small cart seemed to ride down the canyon wall. This is impossible. The cart landed next to me, pulled by a donkey. Within the cart was Merlin, Chuck, and a fox.

"What are you doing here, Merlin? Have you sent this poor little lady her to torture her?"

"I don'ts hurt anyone, she is here fer a trial, they ain't any a yer business. Now sets her down," Chuck directed.

Elaine walked up to the cart and greeted Merlin. She did not know of the others so she asked, "Who are your companions?"

"Elaine, it is not for me to introduce you. This is Chuck's party. I must abide by his rules."

"But, Merlin, aren't you the greatest mage in the entire kingdom?"

"That I am, but there are others with greater powers than mine. Until I am told otherwise, I can't tell you why we are here or anything else."

Chuck waddled over to my side. "An whatcher doing here anyways? This is an area most folks dun't knows about. How did yer gets here?"

"Chuck, I wish I could tell you. I found Elaine in Canterbury and thought I was taking a short cut to the castle. I don't know how we came to be here."

"And, you have told no one else?" Chuck inquired.

The ground hog was getting testy. I've never known him to be so cross. He is most often the happiest of beings. Why had his demeanor changed so drastically?

Merlin approached us and whispered to Chuck softly, but I could hear. "What are we to do? We were not counting on Fiona being attacked, nor on the appearance of Elaine and Morganna."

"Wall, now I gots to ponder this fer a while. I be set over thar by the cart. I'll gets back to you quick-like."

The rain and winds threatened again. I went to the cart to find larger and heavier shawls to protect Elaine and me. Merlin found a covering for Fiona. So, we were prepared for inclement weather. I watched as Chuck appeared to be speaking to the donkey. To my knowledge, the animal could not talk. At least I never heard him.

Finn walked over to Merlin, saying, "Let me hold her, I'll protect her."

The wizard was hesitant but looked into the eyes of the fox and realized he would never harm Fiona. The fox trampled down some weeds, and laid upon them, his body curved to hold the falcon. Merlin set the bird beside Finn and he wrapped his full white tail around her.

Chapter 15

Chuck

"Wall, the fust two went purty well, but I don'ts know what ter do now. It's clear she got rid of her demons, but I knows what ther Council of Ancients will say. Punish her. But it weren't her fault, she were attacked."

"Merlin, hows you with the council? Yer had lots of dealins with, ain't ya?"

"Yes, more often than I wished. Why do you ask?" the sorcerer replied.

"I pose yer know I kind had a not so nice dealins with em. Buts, I gots ter ask em what ter do bouts Fiona. She didn't finish, but is tis clear to me, she did vanquish her fears."

"She certainly did, never complained about her wounds. Bled a lot, but she never made a peep." The mage frowned.

"Wait a minute. You said, 'She didn't finish, but it is clear to me she did vanquish her fears.' How come your language got so proper suddenly?"

"I wasn't always a ground hog, you know."

"I can accept that, I was once a fawn. So, who are... what are you?"

"Understand, Merlin, I am not at liberty to impart the council's plans. A least, not at this time."

"Quite so, I shall not press you further. But, I must admit, my interest is more than piqued."

A loud rumbling assaulted my ears. The sky grew dark, the wind howled, and from the sky a waterspout formed. It twisted about itself, thin, not dropping anything. It just howled and danced across our path. The howling grew louder by the minute. We could not speak to each other.

We scurried for cover. Strangely though the sound was near to deafening, the wind normally found here was still. Nothing moved. Then the sound grew to a pitch that assaulted us.

"Dad burn it, the poor donkey is out in this," Chuck said. Jest then the tent flap was pushed aside and Amadeaus entered. I knowed he was vexed with me. And he had every right to be. He walked to our little circle where we had gathered to protect ourselves. He pushed his head into my shoulder and took me from the others. I hoped he would be in a better mood. He shook free of the cloth and spoke directly into my ear.

He said very softly, but still authoritatively, "You realize, Chuck, this mission is a loss."

"But, Sire, there is no way I could have known Fiona would be attacked. And she will mend quickly." I talked to him with my nose up to his ear.

"That is correct, yet you should have prepared for all manner of weather. It is known to be quite windy here. Is it not?"

"Yes, and we were prepared for the chill and the wind. But this is unlike anything I've ever seen. Ever!"

Amadeaus nodded, saying, "Chuck, you know we expected more from you. However, I suppose since you had never before seen this bizarre weather you could not have briefed me on the situation."

"Yes, Sire. And I am deeply sorry, I forgot about you out in the rain and wind. Very, very sorry. Please forgive me."

"It is not of any consequence. I could have stopped it at any time, but I wanted to know how and why it occurred."

"I don't know what to say. How can I help?"

"Start a fire. A big one. Whoever did this will not be deterred by a small blaze."

Going back to our group, with hand signals I conveyed that we were to build a large fire. Finn ran from the others and proceeded to gather twigs.

Merlin came to me and Amadaeaus. "Gentlemen, I now know who you both are. Why do we not create a huge fire by magic?"

"Oh, you think you know who we are, eh?" I placed my paw on the wizard's shoulder and indicated he was not to speak. Merlin bowed his head and stepped several paces away from us.

Strangely, the violent weather eased its howling, and the rain stopped. There was no longer a need for a fire. The silence was profound. Never have I been in such a massive soundless situation.

From the darkened cloud high above us came a very well-dressed man. He walked over to our group, huddling together, and placed some kind of restraint on Elaine and Finn. Fiona flew as he approached. The man was somewhat short and quite muscular, dressed in a long robe that was finely embroidered with tiny white flowers on a regal purple.

Merlin rushed back to Amadeaus and me and told us what had occurred. Amadeaus looked up at the departing priestess and fox. They seemed to be floating in a bubble of some sort. The enclosure appeared to be made of glass.

Finn growled and snapped at the encasement they found themselves in. To no avail. Elaine cried out, "Help us."

Amadeaus stood on his hind legs and began to transform into a human-like man. I was dumbfounded. I never had seen a transformation of one so high in the Ancient Council, let alone the highest member. As a man Amadeaus was somewhat unremarkable. He wore the cloak of a cleric, though modest, it was a brilliant white.

His features were commonplace. Blue eyes, a chubby face that seemed to want to smile, but never quite made it. He was a solemn man, not given to levity. His voice was soft, but with an authority that could not be ignored.

Merlin knelt beside me and whispered, "Chuck, what do you make of this? Should we be worried?"

"Nah, jest cause he's here dunt mean nuthin, fer us anyhow. We dunt matter that much. Sides, we are gonna retire."

"Well, then why is he here and in his true form?" The wizard was both fearful and worried. Not only for himself, but for Elaine and Finn.

"Chuck," the highest one said.

"Do you have any idea where they are going? We must retrieve them before midnight."

"Wall, the only place I ever seed him was near that big mausoleum ahind the monastery."

"Good," he replied.

"Sire, how exactly are we to address you?" the sorcerer asked.

"What is your name?"

"Chuck, you know my name, as do you, Merlin, if you think about it."

The wizard scowled and pulled at his beard. "You? You are Amadeaus!" Merlin stood paralyzed, his mouth agape and began to weep.

"Whatcher crying about" I asked.

"He's a feller jest like us." Merlin stared wide-eyed at me.

"I-I don't know what to say."

"Fear not, I am here to help," Amadeaus said.

"We must hasten and find them before midnight. For if he has them, I fear we will never find them."

"You need have no further reason to fear. Finn is one bright fox. He will escape that fool's clutches and take Elaine with him." I was proud of the lad he'd become more than I expected, and I know he is capable of saving the High Priestess.

Amadeaus nodded to us, and Merlin and I loaded the cart. The sorcerer leaned over as we worked side by side. "How are we to get back to the mausoleum, who is going to pull the cart?"

"Ya crazy old coot, it is past time for you to retire. Amadeaus will handle our transportation." Sometimes I wonder at the old man. He'd forgotten more than half of the magic, he learned. I scratched my head with my paw.

"Now gets inter ther wagon, and I'll finish up."

I grabbed what little was left of our campground and climbed into the wagon. *Poor old Merlin, I thought as he climbed aboard and arranged his clothing about his frail body.*

All were now seated in the wagon, save Amadeaus. He lifted his arms, palms up, as I'd seen Morganna, and Elaine do when they wished to rise the mist surrounding Avalon. Must be something ya sort of know from being a priestess.

As the council's master lowered his arms and placed his palms against his thighs, the cart rose in the air. The waterspout was gone, and not a single wisp of my fur was out of place as we left the canyon. I were sorta holding me breath, cause I were jest a mite scared. Merlin had been holding his far longer than I and was now turning blue. I gulped and shook the mage. He gasped and inhaled a great breath. Musta been something more in that breath than oxygen, cause he now appeared as the greatest mage in all of Britain, as I had known him for many years.

Amadeaus reached around his shoulders. "Have no fear, Merlin, I too know moments of forgetfulness. It come with age, a warning to us not to waste time on foolish things. We five will save this situation and all will be well."

Chapter 16

I was more than a little confused. Why are we floating around in a bubble? I don't even know anything about the woman. Does she know I am not a real fox? Well, if we are going to die, I suppose it doesn't matter.

"Ma'am," I said, hoping she would understand me, "Will you please tell me what we are doing in a bubble?"

"Oh, my goodness, you aren't just a woodland creature, are you?"

"No, my lady, I was once a baron's son. A foolish lad at that. Now I am part of something I barely understand. Do you know how we can return to Merlin, Chuck, and Fiona?"

"If it weren't for this glass globe we are in, my answer would be yes. But, I have never seen such a thing. If we could break it, we might fall to the ground, however we can't even see the ground. It would be foolish to take such a chance. Have you any way to commentate with the others?"

"No, not really, but Fiona always finds me if I am in trouble. But right now she is hurt and I don't know how badly."

"We have to do something. The man behind this is horrible."

The globe rose suddenly. We went higher and higher, then began to slowly descend, until we could finally see the ground. I saw the monastery, the graveyard, and a big building. Elaine drew in a sharp gasp.

"What is it that frightens you so?" I said.

"Oh, please don't let him lock me in that stone prison again. It's beautiful on the inside, but it is in fact a grave."

"Why did he put you in there?" I could feel the hair on the scruff of my neck rise. It seems this priestess was not cut of the same cloth as Morganna. The encasement landed gently on the grass in front of the stone building. At once the bubble burst. In front of us was the man who put us in the globe.

"What do you want with us?" I demanded. Before us stood the elegantly dressed man. He grinned a strange smile, almost sinister, as he whipped around to speak directly to us.

"From you, fool fox, nothing. You are collateral damage, nothing more. Elaine knows what it is I desire. Don't you, my lady?" he said sarcastically.

"Look." She stood in front of him with authority I'd not noted before. "I don't know or care what it's you want. We are leaving, and you, however powerful you think yourself to be, will not stop us."

"That, my dear, is not quite so. I have more power than any mage in existence."

"Merlin, I am sure would contest that," Elaine replied.

"And I am equally certain he would not."

I saw he was not paying any attention to me thus he did not notice as I crept away. I found myself behind the massive Glastonbury Monastery and heard a strange hissing noise. Creeping back into the bushes, I remained hidden until I saw the source of the noise. Looking up from my hiding place, I noted a cart much like the one I rode in earlier. As it came closer, I saw it was not merely like the one I knew, it was the very same. Within the wagon was Chuck, Merlin, Morganna, and my beloved Fiona. I raced to her side. Not being with her in times of danger cut me to the core.

Chuck called out to me, "Hey thar, Finn, hows comes you is here? Whar is Elaine?"

"Don't know for certain, but I think that Breasel fellow took her in that big stone building back there," I said, pointing at the Mausoleum.

Merlin interjected, "Has he made any demands? What does he want?"

"He did sorta say what he wanted, but didn't specify." Finn wrinkled his snout to show his discomfort.

Chuck was becoming more and more agitated by the minute. "What? He did but he didn't. What does that mean?"

"He said Elaine knows what he wants, but didn't clarify exactly what it is." Merlin stepped out of the cart and joined us.

"I think I know what it is that he wants."

"Do tell, Master Wizard," Chuck responded.

"No need for snarky comments, Chuck. This is a serious matter," Morganna said.

"Please tell us, Merlin," I interjected.

"Does it have to do with Avalon or Camelot?"

"No," Merlin replied.

"It covers more than our kingdom. If Breasel acquires this book he shall have control over any priestess or wizard throughout the entire world. Morganna, do you recall when Elaine was made High Priestess, and you had to relinquish the title?"

"I do. She was made High Priestess without any of the formal protocol. She was required to learn nothing, just made her High Priestess. I was angry for a time, but as the historian, though not really my position, I have done what is required."

Merlin patted her shoulder and smiled down upon her. "Yes, lass, your commitment is well appreciated. You have gone well above what is required. I'm very proud of you." He hugged her gently and gave her a quick wink.

Chapter 17

Breasel

These fools annoy me. If it weren't for the book, I wouldn't bother with them. But the power is a sweet that can't be untouched. The grimoire is a book that can give me all I want, forever.

Who does she think she is, to dare confront me? After all I have done for her, over the many years I followed her, you would think she would show me some gratitude.

"Now, my dear, you know what it is I seek. Take me to the location. Consider you could have the world at your feet if you choose to ally with me. If not stay where you are and have nothing."

"I do not know what it is that you desire so. I can't take you to the location if I do not know what you want," Elaine replied. She is shaking with fear and now is crying.

"Elaine," I demanded.

"Cease this crying and take me to the book." She wiped her tears with the sleeve and drew herself erect. A posture of authority.

"How many times do you have to be told, I don't know what you are talking about?" She looked haughty and glared directly at me.

Suddenly a cart appeared. In it were Merlin, Morganna, and an elegantly dressed tall man I'd never seen before. His suit was so white it appeared to glow.

As the wagon drew nearer, Merlin jumped out with the vigor of a young man. "What are you doing, Breasel? What do you think will happen if the Highness of the Council hears of this?"

"You, old man," I replied.

"That is just a faux name to keep wizards in line. It's a myth to frighten young novices into good behavior."

The well-dressed man stepped out of the conveyance. Power exuded from him, as he stepped ever closer to me. It was almost as if he was pushing me back, without raising a hand. I felt powerless and completely under his control.

"Who are you? And what is it that you covet?" he asked in a tone that demanded an answer.

I would not allow myself to be intimidated by a man in a snow-white robe. "I am known as Breasel the Bold and I want the book Elaine is keeping from me."

"And does the book actually belong to you? Who awarded you the book?"

"It's a spell book and Merlin gave it to Elaine, uh, me."

Merlin strode over to me, saying, "Breasel, you are a liar. I never gave you anything other than my distain."

"Merlin, you are elderly and you forget the things you gave me. Elaine took it from me. Remember?"

"I may be old, Breasel, but I suffer not from a lack of memory. I can't recall, however that which never occurred."

The short, well-muscled man pushed the wizard behind him. "I also recall my chosen mage referred to you as Breasel the Weasel. How did that title come to be yours? Refresh my memory."

"And just who are you, that dares to question me? I have many skills. You have no power over me."

Merlin was laughing at me. His hand covered his mouth as he snickered.

The short man exhibited not sign of either anger or pleasure. Who is he?

"Sir, you owe me at the very least your name. What is reason for your presence here?"

"While I am not obligated to answer your query, I shall give my name, You may recall it from your days within your training as a wizard. It is certain you were warned what would befall you should you not change your behavior. I am Grand Master, the Highest of the Ancient Council."

No, it can't be. That was just a tale to frighten the novices. "Grand Master, it is indeed an honor to meet you. Certainly, you realize I am the true owner of the grimoire. Would you please direct Elaine to relinquish it to me?"

The stocky fellow, dressed somewhat like a cleric, crossed his arms.

"Breasel, you are not the true owner of the book, nor is there anyone who is owner. The book is not given, only entrusted to one who will protect it, until I deem the time is right to place it in the custody of another. It was never entrusted to you, nor will it ever be."

"But, Sire, I have worked long and hard for this sacred book. I should be entrusted with it. I have mastered skills that others have not even thought of. I shall be compensated. You should give me the book as I have earned it. Who are you to tell me what to do? Why should I even pay any attention to you?" *I was so certain there was no Grand Master.*

"Breasel, Breasel, you know that is not the truth. You have scammed and wheedled your way since you were thrown out of the school. You have no right to call yourself wizard," the Grand Master replied.

"But, Sire, I learned all on my own. Should I not be recognized for my talent alone?" I asked. *It is easy to see this was not going to be in my favor.*

"Stealing and sneaking around is not the proper way to obtain knowledge. You have been warned time and time again. Thus, it is your time to face up to what you have done."

I see no future.

~ ~ ~

Elaine

"Merlin, come quick," I cried out.

"There is something wrong with Fiona!"

"She was fine just moments ago. What has happened?" he replied.

"She was, until I gave her some water from that jug," I said, pointing to the dark vessel that stood on the table.

As the attention was diverted from Breasel, I noted he was trying to escape. He moved slowly toward the edge of the clearing. But Amadeaus stopped him before he reached the forest. With a simple wave of his hand, the culprit was bound tightly against a large tree. He began to sob until his shoulders shook.

"Perhaps, little man, you are thirsty. Here, have some of this cold dark water."

"No, I am not thirsty," Breasel said, turning his face to the side, so Amadeaus could not reach his mouth with the vessel.

"Now I doubt that. It is very hot here in this canyon."

"No, I am not in need of a drink."

"Never let it be said, I did not care for my prisoners. You will drink. Now."

The fool shook his head violently. His nose hit the jug and splashed the very dark liquid onto Amadeaus's white robe.

Merlin came to my side as I held Fiona gently in my hands. "What do you think caused this?" he asked. He examined the falcon and noted there were no grave injuries.

"Have no fear, she will survive. I know the cause for this illness. The water has been tainted. This is not plain water. There is poison in it."

Poison? Could I be the perpetrator of this foul deed? I looked into the container and noted it was far darker and thicker than what I put into the well.

"Elaine," Amadeaus called to me, "I believe you have some part in this, but this fluid is much darker and of greater viscosity than what you used. Is this not so?"

I hung my head. I was guilty, but not to this degree of putridness. Yet, I knew there was a price to pay.

"Sire, you are correct, but I did not use anything this dark or thick. My only intent was to make Morganna a little sick, not to become as violently ill as she became. I had no idea the well ran to Camelot as well as our isle. I would never intentionally gravely harm anyone. I was jealous, not murderous."

Merlin took the bird from my hand and placed his other on my shoulder. "Elaine, I'm sorry you did this. You must repent and serve, in order that you might be exonerated."

"I will do whatever is asked of me. I promise. I am terribly sorry. Morgana, you know I would never seriously harm you."

"I know, Elaine, but sometimes you fail to take into consideration the severity of your actions," she replied.

Amadeaus came to my sides as he tried to wipe the offending stain from his robe. The mark remained. "Elaine, I know you are not the true culprit, but you have harmed many."

"I know. I know, some even died. I feel awful. Is there any way you can return their lives?"

"I can, but you must assist me, as part of your penance. Do you understand?"

"Whatever you bid, Grand Master, I will do." I was truly relieved. I could have been banished or even jailed. What I had done was punishable to the gravest degree.

Amadeaus looked at this robe. A stain that could not be removed was to him a grave offense. The man was always impeccable, nothing to mar his appearance. He placed his hand over his face and vanished.

What am I to do? Where has he gone? I turned to Merlin, who was tending Fiona.

"Merlin, how is she? Will she be all right?" I'd known this brave little bird only a short time, but I felt that she was dear to me.

The wizard had wrapped her in a soft blanket and was holding her gently. I looked at her and saw she was awake. I spoke softly. "Merlin believes he can cure you, and I am praying for the same. Get well, little Fiona. We all need you."

Merlin spoke up. "She will survive, but we must get back to my workroom, that I might make her more comfortable and have at hand the medicine she needs."

"I agree, but how are we to get there? Amadeaus is gone."

Just then, I heard the soft tinkling of a windchime. Immediately Amadeaus appeared before us. His robe again sparkled.

I now held the bird, and the sorcerer moved over to Amadeaus asking, "How are we to return to Camelot?"

The Grand Master smiled, raising a single brow. "Have all you wizards not remembered your powers? Perhaps peace has dulled your abilities? How do you wish to travel? Walk, in a bubble, in a cart? I know, let us fly. Remember you can do that." He has a sense of humor, laughing as he towered over the six-foot Merlin.

I felt like a fool. It is as if a cloud passed over me and took my memory. Will I ever be able to access what I was taught?

Merlin hung his head. I am sure he felt the same as I. The only difference is he has been taught far more than I.

"Grand Master." I dared to speak for everyone.

"Sire, I think we all agree we will fly."

~ ~ ~

Chuck

Wall, I wonder whats gonna happen now? No way thet sweet little bird is gonna have her trial counted for. 'Tain't her fault though. Mabe the Grand Master could do sumpin bout it?

"Er, Grand Master, ya surpos ya could do sumpin fer the little lady Falcon? I mean she ain't hurt thet bad. And thet big bird grabbed her tight. She still a mite ascared. But, I think she dun good. She learned to face her fear of the canyon, and if I unnerstan right, thet were the object of this mission."

"I have taken that into consideration and will inform the council. I must leave you for a short period of time. I shall be back within the hour." Without a goodbye to anyone he vanished.

"Wall, my friends, I'm not sure if there is any more to this situation. So, let's go back to ter the castle and think a mite about this. Okays? I guess ya all agrees, so off we gos to Merlin's workroom."

Not a word was spoken as we flew from the strange canyon. Within a very short time we were all in the workroom.

Morganna sighed and held Fiona close to her breast. The falcon moved, Morganna loosened her grip and laid her on the table and stroked the bird's feathers.

"I dunt mean ter interrupt you ladies, but I found sumpin yer jest mite be interested in."

They looked at me with vacant eyes. As if they wer a single person, they said at the exact same time, "What?"

"Wall, ya member hows ya gots mad, Morganna, and tossed yer spell book out the winder?" The Priestess Morganna's eyes widened and her mouth fell open, "Did, did you find it?" she asked.

"Yep, I did, and I noticed sumpin different than when I first saw this book. It's bigger by a lot. And the cover is a little wrinkled, guess from the marsh water. Yer best read it, Morganna. I cain't read, ya know. I hed it awhile but hearing thet fool wizard talk bout the Grimoire like it wer sumpin valuable, I figgered it jest might be valuable. The Grimoire is a book, right?"

"Not just a book but The Book. Please may I have it?" Morganna said.

She was excited and a little ascared. Sos I waddled over ter her whar, she set on the bench at the table. Holding her hands out as if I were handing her the world.

~ ~ ~

Elaine

I knew I had a lot to atone for. My memory is not as it was not so long ago. I remember a large group of people were reported as deceased, but I can't recall any funerals. Moving to Morganna's side at the table, in Merlin's quarters, the old man was poring over a large book. He looked up at me and asked, "Elaine, do you remember seeing a dead body? One who had died from this poison?"

I was puzzled, as I had been thinking the same thing. "No, Merlin, I can't even recall that the king told us to be present at a funeral. Surely we would be required to attend such a thing?" Hearing a knock at the door, I looked up and saw Arthur.

"Come in, Arthur."

Merlin said, "Sire, I have been searching all the papers that pertain to this strange illness that has befallen many. Yet, I find no records of their deaths. Is there a reason for this?"

The regent seemed to have no answer to the wizard's question. His eyes grew glazed, and his features and his features contorted with confusion. "Think, Arthur, did you see even one dead person?" Arthur shook his head no.

"Amadeaus must have something to do with this. No mortal could have done this," Merlin declared.

"Who is Amadeaus? What does this new person have to do with this? And why was I not informed?" Arthur demanded.

Our king was becoming irate. I ventured to explain to Arthur what our situation was, the poison, the water, the illness, all of it. "Sire, please be seated; this is long and complicated. And, I am afraid, I too have a part in it." Arthur looked at me as if I'd grown a second head. I knelt before him, my hands on his knees. Something is out of place. To touch a regent without permission was not done. But I did and explained the entire fiasco to him.

"Elaine, I think I grasp the situation. It seems to me your part is minimal. However, it will be up to the Council of the Ancients what your punishment shall be," Arthur said.

~ ~ ~

Amadeaus

I was somewhat surprised by the decision of the council. I feared they would deny Fiona her trial. They did not but applauded her endeavor. She is one plucky little lady.

Now, the only true problems are to cleanse the water, confine Breseal, and raise the 'so-called' dead.

Chuck interrupted my thoughts. "Ah, Grand Master, you gonna tells what ter do now? Merlin wants to retire. Don'ts know fer sure, but I think Finn and Fiona wants ter marry and them being, yer know, kinda different might be a problem." I laughed.

"Don't give it a thought, Chuck. The council has erased all wrong. Even the dead shall arise."

"But how? Not even the monks can do that."

"My dear Charles, that is not for you to know. Just be assured all will be well."

~ ~ ~

Merlin

I do not know why Amadeaus has called us to hear the words of the council. However, I am not fearful. Amadeaus is the Grand Master of the highest standing. He has presided over all for centuries.

Though I told them I was not afraid, I still am apprehensive.

Upon hearing a knocking at the doorway, I noted it was Arthur seeking entrance. "Good day, my King, I'm sorry but I can't admit you."

"Can't admit me? This is my castle. I shall enter whenever and wherever, I choose."

Nearly in the same moment, Amadeaus appeared. "Your Highness, I understand the castle is yours. However, in view of the situation, Merlin's workroom is mine for only a day."

"A day?" Arthur glowered. "How can I deed a single room for one day only?"

"Fear not, Sire, there need be no documentation," the Grand Master said.

Arthur was angry. "Merlin, please come out here and explain this so-called 'situation.'"

I rose from the worktable and joined my king at the doorway. "Arthur, no one wants to take any portion of yours. Please understand this meeting is for those of us who possess magic. Furthermore, if this congregation is not allowed here in my quarters, you will lose more than a single room." As I'd never told the regent a falsehood, Arthur turned from the door and walked down the corridor.

Turning to rejoin the others at the table, I saw Amadeaus was sitting at the head of the table in my chair. He extended his arm and indicated I was to sit on his left. *This must be how Arthur feels.*

Amadeaus cleared his throat and struck the oaken table, with the flat of his large hand. Each of us flinched at the sound.

"Well, now that I have your undivided attention we shall begin. The first item is on the retirement of Chuck and Merlin."

I kind of knew this would be discussed, I don't even know what I want to do.

Chuck interrupted, "Waits jest a minute. You ain't sendin me ta some home. I gots plans, ya know."

Amadeaus cleared his throat and crossed his arms. "Would you care to impart those plans to me?"

Chuck was a mite testy. "Listen, Grand Master, I gots lots a friends here. And, sides, I gots me a girlfriend. She's smart as a whip and right purty too."

"I see, Chuck. I suppose you wish to stay here? And what of the woman? Does she return your feelings?"

"Acourse she does. At my age yer don't waste with someone what don't loves ya back."

"I understand, Chuck. Do you wish me to re-animate you to her species?"

"Nah, we gets along jest fine as we is. I wants ter to stay here without all the sponsability."

Amadeaus nodded and turned back to me. "And you, Master Merlin, what is it you desire?"

"Amadeaus, I am not certain what I want or where I wish to be."

Chuck said, "Wall, I tell yer what. Each of us sleep on this fer a night and then we will reconvene in the morning. Thet ceptable to you, Grand Master?"

Amadeaus nodded his consent.

~ ~ ~

Chuck

We dun sleeped on it fer the night and went to the campground by the marsh. We agreed to meet once we waked.

"Wall, my old friend, looks like me en you is all sets," I sezs.

Poor old feller, guess he ain't sure what he wants to be or even whar fer thet matter.

"You know, Chuck, I spent most of the night thinking about what I wanted. When I first became a wizard, so very long ago, I wanted to be a professor like the ones who taught me."

"Wall, dad burn it, man, thets what yer ought ter do then."

"And I think I'd like to travel."

"Thar ya goes. Be an iterant feller, ya know, goes all around and teach others, whatcher knows."

"I think," Merlin said,

"That is what I shall do. Chuck, may I ask you a personal question?"

"Shore, whatcher wanna know?"

"How is it your vocabulary is actually extensive, yet your speech is, er, rather humble?"

"Wall, yer sees, I jest fell in love and I been speaking this way fer centuries. Me Damsel likes me jest the way I am. She makes me feel I'm jest perfect fer her."

"Wall, as you would say, I guess that makes you perfect, I understand," Merlin replied.

"Yep, I thinks we have ther best situation. Nows we have gots to figger a wedding fer them youngens. And, I thinks I know, what kinda future they wants."

Finn approached with Fiona riding on his back and she flew ta me and landed on the large rock whar we usually spoke. *Love the little gell, as if she were my daughter. We was bonded.*

"Wall, little lady, has yer figgered whats gonna wok fer ya?" She fluffed her feathers, then preened them back inter place."

"Chuck, Finn and I would like to start a family."

"So yer wants ter be a mommy. Thet is a great ideer."

As I looked to see what Finn were athinkin, as messenger approached and hands the parchment ter Finn. He reads ther paper and his shoulders drop and he's acryin. All of us rushed to his side.

"What's wrong? Is someone ill?" Merlin asked.

Elaine and Morganna joined us. Elaine knelt beside the fox. "I'm so sorry for your loss, Finn. Unfortunately, that is the way of life. The father gives way to the son."

"Hey," I sez.

"How's come yer knows sumbuddy died?"

"Because I am a seer."

"Yeah, so who's dead? I knowed Lady Elaine fer lotsa time. Didn't know she could see tommara, terday."

Merlin and Fiona looked at each other. Then Fiona flew to Finn's side and pushed her head into his fur.

"I'm so sorry, Finn. Though I've seen the man, I never actually met him. Were you close with your father?"

"No, my dear, and it is something I deeply regret. I resented coming here to Camelot and we rarely spoke to each other. But I have changed from an adolescent to a man," Finn replied.

Merlin interjected, "That you have, young man, and it is a fine adult you've become, and I am certain your father knows as well and he is quite proud of you."

"Shore he is. Dad burn it, I proud of him and I ain't his da."

Then I looks up and sees the king walking kinder fast to our campsite near the marsh. I hollered out ter him.

"Hey, thar Kingness, looks like yer gots sumpin portent to say."

"Yes, I do. Are you the Chuck Merlin told me about?"

"Yep. What's so portent ter bring ya here?"

"I'm looking for the baron's son."

And like he always does, Merlin interjected, "Your Highness, why are you looking for the boy?"

"His father passed away and the boy is now a baron and the title and castle belong to him."

Finn heard the king and said, "Sire, my father and I were not close. I'm certain he did not leave a will."

At once, as usual, Amadeaus appeared before us. He adjusted his robe and sat on the bench at our table. "Have you all considered your future?"

"Yes, we have all thought well about our futures. A plan for each of us," Fiona said.

"Well, before we implement your decisions, the matter of the barony must be dealt with," Amadeaus stated.

Arthur spoke up. "I'm truly sorry for your father's passing, but I must know quickly if Finn is both able and desirous of the position of baron."

"Wall, I wasn't gonna to allow anyone ter disparage, the man I held in my heart to be my son is more than capable. He dun everythin I asked, an he's a quick learner."

Amedeaus nodded, saying, "I agree, Chuck, the lad is my choice as well. What say you, Finn?"

"While I deeply regret not being the son my father could be proud of, I think he would rest easier, if I picked up where he left off. I accept."

"Very good, young man. I too am very proud and pleased you have made this decision," Amadeaus replied. "Now, Morganna, do you understand you are now The High Priestess of Avalon, as you were always meant to be?"

Morganna nodded to Amadeaus and bowed her head in compliance. "Now, Elaine, do you realize you must spend a year and a day traveling with me?"

"I do, Grand Master," she replied and bowed as Morganna had. "Nuff a this jibber gabber. Let's finish this. What about Breasel and the poison?"

Arthur raised his hand. "The water system has been purged and is now safe."

"Yep, your men are right smart fellers. They dun good."

Arthur smiled and asked Amadeaus, "What of Breasel. Should he be hanged?"

"No, Arthur," the Grand Master replied.

"If he were to be killed he would simply reappear in another form. Therefore, he shall remain where he is. The tree will surround him and he will become part of the ancient oak."

~ ~ ~

Finn

"Fiona, this is a strange set of circumstances. While I shall miss my father, I knew him only as I was a child, so I resented his orders. Strangely, I do not feel as I suppose I should. The barony is a stroke of good fortune. We shall have an income and a place to live. It is not as grand as Camelot, but far better than where I was born."

"Yes, I understand your conflicting feelings, but how are you going to run a barony if you are a fox?"

"Fiona, have you forgotten what we stayed up all night talking about, how we could be re-animated?"

"Of course, I remember, but we aren't retirement age."

"I thought you fell asleep against my shoulder. We don't have to be old to have our lives together."

Epilogue

Merlin

Amadeaus had done all he promised. He and Elaine are already on the year and a day journey. Morganna moved into the High Priestess's quarters. Both Finn and Fiona were exotically happy. Likewise, Chuck and Damsel were prepared to spend their lives together.

I had to admit it seemed as if Amadeaus had ordered the perfect day for a double wedding. The sun shone brightly, and the wind was a gentle breeze. Finn's lanky boyhood had been molded into a handsome red-haired man. Chuck stood beside him, his paws clasped over his ample belly. Both looked down the chapel aisle at their brides.

Damsel could barely contain herself, she wiggled trying to slow to Fiona's pace.

Fiona walked slowly and majestically, her train made of a delicate lace, ruffled in the gentle breeze. Her gown Amadeaus had procured from the most talented seamstress, was a work of art. Her long dark hair shone like polished ebony. I've never seen a more beautiful bride.

I was just about to the part of the ceremony where the couples say their vow when Arthur stood and said with a sneer, "Merlin, you can't marry these four."

"Any why can I not do so?" I asked, as I had previously married many other couples.

The attendees grew deadly silent. They all stared at their regent. Within the all-encompassing stillness, Arthur began to laugh. Everyone was confused. He continued to laugh, louder then louder still. The entire congregation remained quiet. Arthur ceased his laughter and walked swiftly up the aisle. There he embraced Chuck, Damsel, Finn, Fiona, and me.

Why? I wondered. What was behind his anger?

Apparently, nothing as he whispered in my ear, "A baron and his wife must be married by a king. I couldn't embarrass Chuck and his lady, so I denied them all."

"But, Arthur, you are a king. You can marry them."

"I can and I shall."

My dear readers we must remember, we are all the same but quite different. Some are happy in their state as Chuck and Damsel. Some strive to seek a higher station, as Morganna. Some must pay the price of their folly, as Elaine. And, some wish to love and build a happy family, as Finn and Fiona.

If you enjoyed reading this as much as I enjoyed writing it, please leave a review on Amazon.

FOX TALES

Two Tales of Love Mark of the Fox

Can an enchanted fox and a scarred prince follow the predestined course the Druids have set for them? They fight against the constraints of royalty, but in the end the falconer becomes a willing regent and the fox, his more- than-willing wife.

The Fox and the Swan

To save her family, a girl becomes a swan. The man she loves is enchanted by a witch into a fox. Can the pair unite as humans and save her family? True love triumphs over evil with the aid of a druid, a bishop, and a goddess.

Available on Amazon: **FOX TALES**

THE CRIMSON VIXEN

The preordained couple meet when Leigh discovers an orphaned fox and keeps her as a secret companion. In time it is revealed his Kit is also a fierce female pirate. The Druids determine the pair are destined to rule Ireland. As a fox she is clever. As a woman she is enchanting. Can Leigh set aside his devotion to King Arthur to be with the woman of his dreams?

Available on Amazon: **THE CRIMSON VIXEN**

FOX TALES II

Two tales will enchant and bring to you the joy of magic, faith, courage, and the most powerful force in the universe: Love Can Shawn save himself and his friends from the grasp of the most foul? Can Merlot and LaRoux follow their preordained paths to save church and country?
Available on Amazon: **FOX TALES II**

THE FOX AND THE MERMAID

Can a woman, who is actually a seal, and a fox, who might be a man, overcome a man who is an ancient Questing Beast?
Only when those afflicted can realize they must cooperate in order to overcome evil do they prevail.
This story focus is upon loyalty, teamwork, and trust.
Available on Amazon: **THE FOX AND THE MERMAID**

THE FOX AND THE RAVEN
(novella)

Can a fox and a raven help to save the life of King Arthur?
Somehow the King is being poisoned. Camelot may lose its ruler.
Merlin, the king's adviser, gets a strange group of animals to uncover the mystery.
Available on Amazon: **THE FOX AND THE RAVEN**